THE ONE WHO

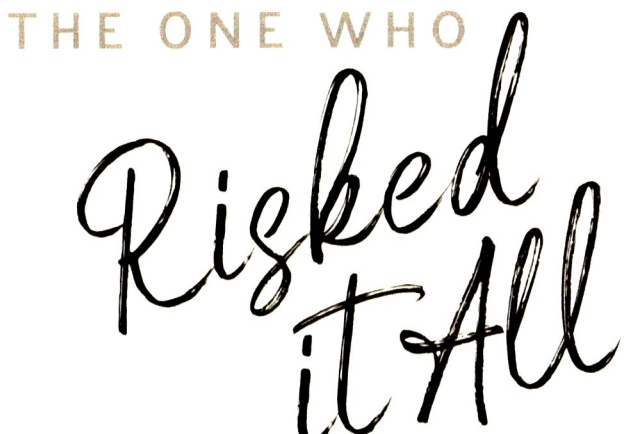

Risked it All

SECOND CHANCE FIRE STATION
Book Four

TARA GRACE ERICSON

Edited by Editing Done Write
Cover Design: Jess Mastorakos
Cover Photo: Lindsay Nickel Photography,
Red Deer, Alberta, CA
Cover Models: Mark and Kristen Boutros

Paperback ISBN-13: 978-1-949896-72-5
Ebook ISBN-13: 978-1-949896-71-8

To the boy who walked away and broke my heart because your parents didn't like me.
Your loss.
PS: My husband says "Thank you!"

"For God has not given us a spirit of fear, but of power and love and self-discipline."

2 TIMOTHY 1:7

Contents

CHAPTER 1

Elijah

I thought about skipping the vow renewal. That I'd even considered missing it probably made me a bad brother and a terrible person. But what else was new?

I was glad Nathan and Rebecca had worked through all their issues–with more than a little help from me, thank you very much. My little pep talk with my big brother was exactly what he needed to pull his head out of his you-know-where. But that didn't mean I wanted to sit and watch them get all gooey-eyed over each other.

"Well, if it isn't Minden's finest pyromaniacs–I mean, firefighters," I quipped, striding up to Bryce, Jake, and Matteo as they lounged on one of the park benches. The autumn breeze ruffled my hair, carrying the scent of barbecue and laughter from the nearby pavilion.

Bryce was another captain at the department, like my brother, and Jake was his best friend. The two were practically inseparable. Matteo was their rookie. He'd been around for almost two years, so calling him a rookie wasn't exactly accurate anymore, but he was still the newest guy on the team.

Bryce rolled his eyes. "Har har, Eli. Just because you can't resist playing with matches doesn't mean the rest of us have a death wish."

"Hey now," I protested, clutching my chest in mock offense. "I'll have you know I haven't set anything on fire in at least..." I pretended to count on my fingers. "Twelve hours."

Jake snorted. "Yeah, and that's only because you've been on duty."

The firefighter/firestarter joke was a long-running bit at the station, ever since I caught the grill on fire that one time. Well, and that other time with the microwave noodles. But no one had seen that happen.

I was pretty sure, at least.

I couldn't help but grin, my gaze wandering to the

festive scene unfolding under the pavilion. The trees surrounding us were a riot of reds and golds, leaves dancing on the breeze like nature had decided to provide the confetti for the party. Strings of twinkling lights crisscrossed overhead, casting a warm glow on the faces of friends and family gathered to celebrate my brother's vow renewal. The ceremony at the church had been small and intimate, but it seemed like the whole town was here to celebrate now.

Considering how much the entire population of Minden had been whispering about the separation, it was only right that they came to affirm the newly-reunited couple. Nathan hated all the speculation. I, on the other hand, wasn't new to that kind of scrutiny. The town had certainly done its fair share of chattering about my indiscretions—real or imagined—over the years.

"You know," I mused, leaning against the back of the bench beside them, "I'm starting to think these lovebirds are just rubbing it in our faces now. I mean, who needs two weddings? Actually, who needs a wedding at all?" I amended with a smirk.

Bryce, who had fallen head over heels for his high school bestie when she came back to town the spring before last, chuckled. "Spoken like a true bachelor. Some of us actually enjoy settling down, you know."

I arched an eyebrow. "Okay, okay. Don't forget to take your dentures out before bed tonight, Grandpa."

Jake nearly choked on his drink, and I felt a surge of satisfaction. It was moments like these, trading barbs with my fellow firefighters, that made me feel most at ease. But as I watched the celebrating crowd, a familiar ache settled in my chest. I pushed it aside, plastering on my trademark grin.

"Well," I said, clapping Matteo on the shoulder, "I'm going to see if I can't rescue some of those cupcakes before Alex sticks his fingers in them all. Y'all have fun."

As I sauntered toward the pavilion, I allowed myself a moment to imagine a different life, one where I wasn't just the charming, quick-witted younger brother, but something more. Then I shook it off, determined to lose myself in the celebration and the comfort of my easy banter. After all, wasn't that what I did best?

I wove through the crowd, my ears perking up as I caught the familiar gruff tone of my father's voice. Instinctively, I slowed my pace as I passed out of his line of sight.

"I'm glad you came to reason, Nathan. I knew you'd do the right thing and stand by your family."

"Thanks, Dad. I know it wasn't easy for you to stand by and give us time to sort it out. But we needed it." I could see the profile of Nathan's face tucked behind the wooden column as I eavesdropped.

"Well, now I just need your brother to get his act together," Dad grumbled, his words piercing through the cheerful chatter around us. "When are you going to talk some sense into him?"

I winced, my fingers tightening around my drink. Of course, Dad would be harping on about me to Nathan. Golden boy Nathan, with his perfect life and his perfect wife.

"Dad, come on," Nathan's voice was soft, placating. "Eli's doing fine. He's got a good job, he's—"

"Running around like a frat boy," Dad interrupted. "He needs to grow up, settle down. Like you did."

I swallowed hard, fighting the urge to step out and defend myself. But what would I say? That I was perfectly happy with my life? I wasn't even sure that was true anymore.

My gaze drifted across the pavilion, and suddenly, there she was.

Carla. My breath caught in my throat as I watched her laugh with my sister-in-law, her dark hair catching the late-afternoon sun. She looked... Man, she looked beautiful.

Memories flooded back, unbidden. The way her eyes used to crinkle when she smiled at me. The softness of her hand in mine as we walked through the halls. The electricity of our first kiss, hidden behind the bleachers of the football field.

She glanced up, catching my gaze for a brief moment, and it was like a jolt straight to my heart.

I wanted to go to her. To say... what? Sorry for letting my father's stupid feud keep us apart? Sorry for pretending I didn't care all these years?

Instead, I stayed rooted to the spot, caught between the disapproval in my father's voice and the longing that threatened to overwhelm me. Some brave firefighter I was. I could run into burning buildings without hesitation, but I couldn't face my own heart.

I plastered on my best charming grin and turned back toward the rest of the party. There was Mrs. Henderson, our elderly neighbor who'd always had a soft spot for me. "Well, don't you look lovely today! That hat is absolutely fetching."

And by fetching, I meant the mass of feathers and

netting looked kind of like a dead bird dragged in by a hunting dog. But if she liked it, who cared?

Mrs. Henderson giggled like a schoolgirl, swatting my arm. "Oh, Eli, you flatterer! How's that handsome fire chief treating you boys down at the station?"

I launched into a story about our latest drill, gesturing wildly and dropping in just enough innuendo to keep her entertained. But even as I played up the rakish firefighter act, my eyes kept drifting to Carla. She was laughing at something Rebecca said, her head thrown back, exposing the graceful line of her neck.

Heaven help me, I wanted to nuzzle that spot right where her pulse fluttered. I pushed away the entirely over-the-line thought. Why hadn't the pull toward her faded after all these years?

I worked the crowd, moving from guest to guest with practiced ease. It was comfortable, this playboy persona I had worn for so long. Safe. But every time I caught a glimpse of Carla, it slipped just a little. The same way it had when we were in high school.

I was in the middle of regaling Jake's grandmother with a highly-embellished tale of my firefighting heroics when I spotted Nathan and Rebecca off to the side. They weren't doing anything scandalous – just talking quietly, heads bent close together. But the intimacy of it hit me like a sucker punch.

My brother reached up, tucking a stray strand of hair behind Rebecca's ear. The tenderness in that simple gesture made my chest ache. Rebecca leaned into his touch, her eyes shining with a love so deep it was almost painful to witness.

I swallowed hard, suddenly aware of how hollow my own laughter sounded. Was that what I'd been missing? That connection, that...belonging?

For a moment, I let myself imagine what it would be like. To have someone look at me the way Rebecca looked at Nathan. To be able to reach out and touch Carla without worrying about family feuds or disappointed fathers or my own blasted insecurities. Or someone else.

It didn't have to be Carla, obviously. That was why I had tried dating so many different girls. But somehow it never went anywhere, despite the rumors that swirled around town. I'd never so much as made it to the third date with any of the girls I'd taken out.

And as much as I hated to admit it, I was beginning to wonder if it was because none of them were her.

I glanced back toward Carla. The longing was so intense it stole my breath. I pulled myself back to the circle of listeners and jumped into the story my captain, Kyle Parker, was telling.

"...and then I said to the chief, 'Well, if you wanted a hot date, you should've just asked!'" I finished with a wink, covering my momentary lapse with an extra dose of swagger.

But as the group around me erupted in laughter, all I could think was: When did playing the clown stop being enough?

I was saved from my brooding by a tug on my sleeve. I looked down to find my nephew Lincoln grinning up at me, gap-toothed and mischievous.

"Uncle Eli! Guess what?" He bounced on his toes, practically vibrating with excitement.

I crouched down to his level, matching his enthusiasm. "What's up, little man? Did you finally master that backflip I've been teaching you?" Backflip was code for somersault for the five-year-old, but it sounded cooler.

Linc giggled, shaking his head. "Not yet! But I'm gonna stay with Mimi and Papa for two whole weeks!"

"Two whole weeks, huh?" I ruffled his hair, ignoring the twinge in my chest. His older brother,

Alex, had shared the news with me earlier at the church, but I was still surprised. Two weeks with my father, the infamous Harold Wells? Poor kid. "That's quite the adventure. You think Mimi and Papa can keep up with you?" Let's just say, I had my doubts.

"Mimi's gonna teach me how to make her apple pie for Thanksgiving, and Papa said I could help him get the garden ready for next year!" Linc's eyes were wide with anticipation.

I forced a grin, pushing aside memories of my own childhood attempts at gardening with Dad. How nothing I ever did seemed to measure up. Not much had changed in that respect. "Sounds like you've got it all planned out, buddy. Just don't eat so much pie you turn into one, okay?"

As Linc rambled on about his upcoming stay, my gaze drifted across the pavilion. It was like a homing missile, effortlessly finding her in the crowd every single time. Carla. The late-afternoon sun caught her hair. She was laughing at something one of the other guests said, and the sound carried over to me, light and musical.

Before I knew what I was doing, I was on my feet. "Hey, Linc, why don't you go see if your mom needs help with anything? I've got to, uh... check on something."

I made my way toward Carla, heart pounding. What was I doing? This was a terrible idea. But I couldn't seem to stop myself.

"Hey there," I said, aiming for casual and missing by a mile. "Having a good time?"

Carla turned, surprise flickering across her face before she schooled it into a polite smile. "Eli. Yes, it was a lovely ceremony."

"Yeah, it's..." I trailed off, suddenly at a loss for words. How do you make small talk with the woman who still haunts your dreams? "The leaves are nice," I finished lamely, gesturing at the vibrant autumn foliage surrounding us.

Carla raised an eyebrow, amusement dancing in her eyes. "The leaves are nice? Wow, Eli Wells at a loss for words. I should mark this day on my calendar."

I chuckled, relaxing a bit. This was familiar territory – our easy banter, the underlying current of... something more. "What can I say? Your beauty has rendered me speechless."

It was meant to be a joke, part of our usual back-and-forth. But there was too much truth in it, and I saw the moment Carla registered that. Her eyes widened slightly, and she took a small step away from me.

"You can't say—"

"Elijah."

My father's voice cut through the moment like a knife. I turned to see him approaching, his expression a mixture of disapproval and wariness.

"Dad." I nodded, instinctively straightening my posture. "We were just—"

"I'm sure you were," he interrupted, his tone leaving no doubt as to what he thought we were 'just' doing. He turned to Carla, his smile not quite reaching his eyes. "Miss Putnam, I believe your mother was looking for you."

Carla hesitated for a moment, her gaze flicking between me and my father. "Of course," she said finally. "If you'll excuse me."

As she walked away, I felt the weight of everything unsaid hanging in the air between us.

I watched Carla's retreating form, fighting the urge to call her back. My father cleared his throat, and I turned to face him, plastering on my best carefree grin.

"Quite a party, huh, Dad? I was just complimenting Carla on the decorations. Did you know she made the cupcakes?"

He didn't buy it for a second. "Elijah, we've talked about this. The Putnams—"

"I know, I know," I interrupted, unable to keep the edge out of my voice. "Ancient family feud, off-limits, yadda yadda. Can't a guy have a friendly conversation?"

My father's eyes narrowed. "It's more complicated than that."

I knew that. Or at least, I thought I did. But watching Carla all day, seeing her laugh and smile with my family, it was getting harder to remember why we were supposed to stay away from each other. Ever since she and Rebecca became close friends, my world had collided with hers far too frequently, and not at all often enough.

"Look, Dad," I started, trying to find the right words, "I get it. But don't you think it's time to let go of whatever happened in the past? You won't even talk about it. I don't even know why I'm supposed to hate their family, because it's some big secret no one in town will even mention. And this town talks about everything and everyone."

He shook his head, his expression hardening. "There are things you don't understand. Just stay away from them. That's all you need to know."

As he walked away, I was left with a swirling mess of emotions. Frustration at my father's stubbornness. Longing for Carla. And underneath it all, that familiar ache of never quite measuring up.

I glanced around the reception, taking in the happy faces of my family and friends. Nathan and Rebecca, lost in their own little world. My mother, fussing over some flower arrangements. And Carla, across the room, laughing at something Jake was saying.

She caught my eye, and a tiny jolt zinged through my chest. But I forced myself to look away.

Time to move on, Wells. For real this time.

I straightened my shoulders, determined to enjoy the rest of the party without dwelling on what couldn't be. But as I made my way toward Bryce and the guys, I couldn't help but wonder if I was really ready to let go of the past – or if I even wanted to.

CHAPTER 2
Carla

I glanced around my cluttered living room, wincing at the chaos. Stacks of ungraded papers teetered precariously on every surface, threatening to topple at the slightest breeze. Bible verses in colorful calligraphy covered the walls–my chosen version of interior design on a budget. I sighed and plopped down on the couch, pushing aside a pile of laundry to make room for myself. This was not how I pictured my evening – surrounded by work and mess instead of curled up with a good book or hanging out with friends.

I'd spent so much time helping Rebecca prepare for the vow renewal that I'd gotten behind on everything else. And I hated being behind.

But that was just how it was sometimes as a

teacher – always more to do, more papers to grade, more lessons to plan. Maybe I should just quit and become a beach bum.

But the sand gets everywhere, I mused as I blew a strand of hair out of my face and focused on the paper in front of me. My eyes skimmed over the student's handwriting, red pen poised above it.

An hour later, I finished with a flourish—or at least as much of one as you can have when grading essays written by seventh graders. Satisfied with my progress for the evening, I stretched my arms over my head and looked around once again at my messy living room.

I supposed this was why God gave us weekends. Somehow, teaching was the only job where you had to spend time at home preparing to do the work, then actually do the work, then spend time at home evaluating the results of the work. Before starting it all over again for the next lesson.

I shook off those thoughts and headed into the kitchen where dirty dishes were piled high in the sink. I needed to check a few more things off my list before I would feel like I could really relax. As I scrubbed away at them under hot water, my mind wandered back to Eli and our awkward encounter at the vow renewal.

Was he really just being friendly? Or was there something more there? Every time I thought I had moved on from my silly high school crush, he said or did something that had me spiraling back into it.

I shook my head at myself. I shouldn't even be entertaining these thoughts. He was off-limits, and the biggest flirt in town. It was foolish to take anything he said seriously. My beauty rendered him speechless? Please.

I focused on the rest of Nathan and Rebecca's vow renewal. The image of them, beaming and in love, tugged at my heart. I couldn't help but feel a twinge of envy.

They got their happily ever after. Meanwhile, I was still stuck in Singleville, Indiana. Population: me. I was approaching thirty, and I was nowhere near where I expected to be at this point in my life. I loved teaching, but I always pictured myself with a van full of kids, running them to soccer practice.

Sometimes, it was even hard to be around Rebecca and the boys. As much as I loved them, that green-eyed monster was ferocious. Rebecca was my best friend, but I couldn't help but want so much of what she had.

As I reached for the next dish with soapy hands, my mind wandered traitorously to another pair of hands—larger, rougher, belonging to a certain infuriating firefighter.

I shook my head vigorously, banishing the thought. I had to push away those all-too-frequent thoughts of smoldering eyes. How did his cocky grin still give me butterflies, even after all these years? I was hopeless. The mysterious feud between our families loomed large, and though I didn't even know the story behind the feud, ignoring it wasn't an option.

Even if I somehow worked up the nerve to ignore my father's subtle jabs at the Wells family, it had been Eli's dad who put an end to our blossoming teenage romance. And while I'd been crazy enough for him and just rebellious enough to hope we could have a shot anyway? Eli had dropped me like a broken bat after a foul ball.

Then, he'd proceeded to date every girl in the tri-county area over the next ten years. I was not going there. I resorted to turning on a podcast while I finished my dishes to keep my mind occupied.

The next morning, I strode into the teacher's lounge, my game face on.

"Morning, everyone!" I called out cheerily, pouring myself a much-needed coffee.

"Carla!" Mrs. Thompson greeted me. "Are you ready for the big day?"

I flashed her a confident smile, squashing down the panic bubbling in my chest. "Oh, you know me. I've got it all under control." Career day at Minden Rogers High School was no minor event. And this year, I was in charge of it.

"That's Carla," Mr. Dawson chuckled. "Always on top of things."

I laughed along, hoping they couldn't see through my facade. Inside, I was a mess of tangled emotions and unresolved feelings. But out there, I was Carla Putnam: tough, capable, and definitely not running on three hours of sleep from pining over a certain dark-haired firefighter.

I took a deep breath and plastered on my best "I've got this" smile as I walked into the gymnasium. The echoes of excited chatter from students and professionals alike hit me like a wall of sound. Career day had officially begun, and it was absolute chaos.

"Okay, folks!" I clapped my hands, projecting my voice over the din. "Let's get our presenters to their designated areas. Doctors to the left, lawyers to the right, and... where are my accountants?"

A group of individuals in business casual attire raised their hands timidly from the back.

"Perfect! You're by the bleachers. Don't worry, everyone, I promise the kids won't bite... much."

As I navigated through the sea of people, directing traffic and answering a million questions at once, I caught a glimpse of a familiar figure in the corner of my eye. Eli, looking unfairly handsome in his firefighter uniform, was setting up a display with his colleagues.

My heart did a little somersault, and I silently cursed its betrayal. Focus. I was a professional, remember?

But as I turned to help a lost-looking veterinarian find her spot, I couldn't help but steal another glance at Eli. He was laughing at something one of the other firefighters said, his eyes crinkling at the corners in that way that always made me weak in the knees.

"Ms. Putnam?" A student's voice snapped me back to reality. "Where should the police officers go?"

I tore my gaze away from Eli, hoping he hadn't noticed my staring. "Right this way, officers," I said, gesturing toward an empty table near the center of the gym. "Let's put you front and center."

As I led them to their spot, I could feel Eli's eyes on me. The weight of our shared history, the unresolved tension between us, seemed to crackle in the air. But I squared my shoulders and kept moving. I had a job to do, after all, and I'd be a fool if I let my feelings for Eli Wells derail this event.

"Alright, everyone!" I called out, clapping my hands again. "Let's make this the best Career Day MRHS has ever seen!"

I plastered on my best teacher smile as I wove through the maze of career booths. "Well, if it isn't the dream team," I quipped, sidling up to my fellow English teachers, Terry and Melissa. "How're we feeling about being outshone by all these exciting careers?"

Terry clutched his chest dramatically. "Outshone? Never! Who needs firefighters and police officers when you can diagram sentences?"

I snorted, grateful for the easy banter. "Oh yeah, the kids are lining up in droves to learn about the thrilling world of semicolons."

Melissa rolled her eyes. "Speak for yourself. I've got a killer Oxford comma joke that's going to blow their minds."

"Ooh, don't spoil it for me," I teased, my eyes inadvertently drifting toward the firefighters' booth.

Eli was there, gesturing animatedly, probably regaling some poor freshman with a heroic tale.

"Earth to Carla," Terry's voice cut through my thoughts. "You okay there? You looked a million miles away... or maybe just over at the fire department table?" He raised an eyebrow.

I forced my attention back to my colleagues. "Just admiring the, uh, fire safety demonstrations," I lied smoothly. "Very... educational."

Melissa followed my gaze and smirked. "Oh yeah, I'm sure that's exactly what you were admiring."

A flush crept up my neck. "I don't know what you're talking about," I said primly, but my traitorous heart skipped a beat as Eli's laugh echoed across the gym. Missy Harrison, the overly perky math teacher, sidled up to Eli's booth. She twirled a strand of hair around her finger, laughing a little too hard at whatever he was saying.

I shouldn't care. I really, really shouldn't. But a ridiculous pang of jealousy twisted in my gut. This was so unprofessional. I didn't care. Shouldn't care. But the roiling in my belly at the display in front of me was undeniable. After all these years, I still hated seeing him with someone else.

"Looks like someone's getting a private lesson in fire safety," Terry snarked, waggling his eyebrows.

I forced out a chuckle, hoping it didn't sound as strained as it felt. "Well, good for them. Now, who wants to help me wrangle some juniors for a thrilling presentation on the joys of MLA formatting?"

As Terry and Melissa groaned in mock protest, I stole one last glance at Eli. Our eyes met for a split second, and I swore I saw a flicker of... something in his gaze. But then Missy said something, and he turned away, leaving me wondering if I imagined it all.

That night, I slumped onto my couch, surrounded by the familiar chaos of my apartment. Stacks of essays teetered precariously on my coffee table, a silent reminder of another grading marathon still ahead. I should knock a few of them out, but after Career Day, even my muscle aches had their own muscle aches.

I ignored the stack of grading and flipped on an episode of my favorite superhero show instead, absently scrolling my phone during the commercials. I jolted in surprise as it rang in my hand.

"Hey, Carla!" Rebecca's cheery voice filled my ear as my heart rate started to calm. "Just wanted to check in. How was Career Day?"

I cradled the phone between my ear and shoulder, picking at the lint on my couch cushion. "Oh, you know, the usual controlled chaos. Pretty sure I prevented at least three small fires and one potential international incident."

Rebecca laughed. "Sounds like a success then! Nathan and I were wondering if you'd like to join us for dinner this weekend?"

"Ah, the newlyweds want to show off their domestic bliss?" I teased, ignoring the little pang in my chest. "I'd love to, but I've got a hot date with these essays. Maybe next time?"

"Carla," Rebecca's voice softened, "I don't want you to shut me out now that Nathan and I are back together. You know you deserve someone special too, right? You'll find him. "

I forced a chuckle, brushing away the conviction from her gentle reprimand. "Oh please, my love life is about as exciting as watching paint dry. Besides, who has time for romance when there are dangling modifiers to vanquish?"

"I'm serious. Don't shut me out, and don't give up hope."

I pressed my eyes closed and swallowed the lump in my throat. Just a few months ago, I'd been telling Rebecca the same thing. As much as I hated hearing it, I knew she was right. Friendship with the right person had a uniquely gentle way of forcing you to face the truth.

"Thanks, Bex. I won't. When do you leave for your trip?"

She explained their travel plans, and I listened absently.

When we hung up, my eyes drifted to the bible verse framed on my wall: "The Lord is my shepherd, I shall not want."

I stared at those words, my phone forgotten next to me. I knew God would always provide everything I needed. So why was I feeling so discontent lately?

CHAPTER 3

Elijah

The tinkling of the bell above B&J Bistro's door barely registered as I stepped inside, my senses immediately assaulted by the comforting aroma of freshly brewed coffee and warm cinnamon rolls. I inhaled deeply, savoring the familiar scent that always reminded me of lazy Saturday mornings at home. I'd never admit it–even under the most extreme torture–but Norm's cinnamon rolls were even better than my mom's.

My eyes swept the room, taking in the usual suspects: Mr. Jenkins nursing his third cup of joe, the high school gossip squad huddled in a corner booth, and—

A dizzy swoop rolled through my middle. Carla.

She was tucked away at a corner table, her dark

hair catching the morning sunlight streaming through the window. I froze, one foot still halfway to the next step, as if I'd stumbled into an invisible wall.

I could play it cool. I was a firefighter, for crying out loud. I had faced down raging infernos. This was just... Carla.

But even as I thought it, I knew it wasn't true. Carla Putnam had never been "just" anything.

I shifted my weight, suddenly hyper-aware of my uniform. Was my hair sticking up? Did I remember to shave this morning?

I had to get a grip. I wasn't in high school anymore.

My eyes darted to the safety of the counter, where Taylor, the ever-cheerful waitress, was already reaching for my usual order. It would be so easy to retreat, to grab my coffee and bolt. But something kept my feet rooted to the spot, my gaze inexorably drawn back to Carla.

She hadn't noticed me yet, her attention focused on grading papers spread across the table. Even from here, I could see the little furrow between her brows that always appeared when she was concentrating.

I could go say hi. What was the worst that could happen?

Images of our last disastrous encounter flashed

through my mind, followed swiftly by the memory of my father's disapproving scowl.

Right. That's what could happen. This was Minden, and if anyone saw us talking, word would get back to my dad. For all its small-town charm, this place was brutal if you wanted to keep anything on the down-low. Scratch that. There was no such thing as down-low in Minden. Only the... up-high. Was that a thing?

I took a deep breath, squaring my shoulders. I was Eli Wells, for crying out loud. I ran into burning buildings for a living. I'd proven that I could get a date with any girl in town in five minutes flat. Surely, I could handle a simple "good morning" to the girl who'd stolen my heart in study hall all those years ago.

Couldn't I?

Let the town biddies say what they wanted. There was nothing wrong with a conversation, whatever my dad thought.

I plastered on my most charming grin and sauntered over to Carla's table. "Well, if it isn't Minden's favorite teacher," I drawled, leaning casually against the chair opposite her. "Fancy meeting you here."

Carla's head snapped up, her eyes widening in surprise. For a split second, I caught a glimpse of something soft in her expression before her walls slammed back into place. "Eli," she said, her smile guarded. "I didn't realize the fire station was giving its employees such long coffee breaks these days."

I opened my mouth to reply, but before I could get a word out, Taylor appeared at my elbow, coffee in hand. "Here's your usual," she said with a wink, sliding the cup onto the table. "Black coffee." As she turned away, I caught sight of a string of digits scrawled on the side.

Mentally, I groaned.

I watched as Carla's gaze flickered to the cup, her eyebrows lifting slightly. The warmth in her eyes cooled, and she turned back to her papers. "Don't let me keep you from your... admirers," she said, her tone clipped.

Frustration bubbled up inside me. Of course, Taylor would choose today of all days to make a move. Despite the fact that I had already told her I wasn't interested. I considered explaining, but the words died in my throat. What did I care what Carla thought about my love life?

Sure, I would keep telling myself I didn't care.

Instead, I pulled out the chair across from her and sat down, ignoring her startled look. "Actually," I said, leaning forward with a conspiratorial grin, "I was hoping you might save me from the hordes of adoring fans. It's exhausting being this irresistible, you know."

She scoffed, apparently not finding me half as amusing as I did myself. I leaned back in my chair, trying to exude confidence, but my fingers tapped an anxious rhythm on the table. Carla's eyes darted between me and her coffee cup, which she twisted nervously in her hands.

"So," I said, desperate to break the tension, "I see you're still addicted to those cavity-inducing monstrosities." I nodded toward the half-eaten cinnamon roll on her plate.

Carla's lips twitched, fighting a smile. "That cinnamon roll is a Chef Norm special. Worth all the calories and then some. And don't act like you don't want one. It wouldn't kill you to indulge a little now and then, Mr. Black Coffee."

"About that..." Smirking, I leaned in, lowering my voice. "Can you keep a secret?"

She raised an eyebrow, curiosity replacing some of the guardedness in her expression. "I'm listening."

"This"—I tapped my cup—"is actually a pumpkin spice latte. Extra whipped cream."

Carla's eyes widened, and then she burst out laughing. The sound sent a warmth spreading through my chest that had nothing to do with caffeine.

"Are you telling me you have the waitress label your girly drinks as black coffee?"

I grinned, sheepish. "The guys at the station can be pretty merciless. A man's got to protect his reputation."

"Your reputation as what? A teenage girl?" She was still chuckling, shaking her head.

"Hey, I'll have you know this takes serious dedication. I have to remember which cup is which when I order for the whole crew."

As we bantered, I felt some of the awkwardness melting away. But beneath it all, a part of me couldn't help wondering what might have been if things had gone differently all those years ago.

I leaned back in my chair, relishing the easy rhythm we'd fallen into. It was time to steer the conversation somewhere safer, though. "So, speaking of the guys at the station," I said, drumming my fingers on the table, "Nathan and Rebecca left for their trip. Two whole weeks in the Bahamas."

Carla's eyes lit up. "Oh, I know. I actually helped Becca pack earlier this week. I'm so happy for them."

"Yeah, well, someone's gotta hold down the fort." I chuckled. "My parents are watching the boys."

Her eyebrow shot up, a mischievous glint in her eye. "I hope your parents have plenty of coffee. Those three terrors? Oh boy."

I couldn't help but laugh. "I know, right? Dad's already talking about reinforcing the backyard fence."

"Smart man." Carla grinned. "I've seen those boys in action. They're like tiny tornadoes."

As she spoke, she absently tucked a strand of hair behind her ear. The gesture was so familiar, so quintessentially Carla, that it sent a pang through my chest. I was so cooked. One conversation with her and I was a love-sick puppy, desperate for scraps of attention.

"I give it three days before Mom's calling for backup," I said, trying to focus on the conversation and not the way Carla's eyes crinkled when she smiled.

She leaned forward, her voice dropping conspiratorially. "Want to start a betting pool? My money's on day two."

I snorted. "You're on. Loser buys coffee next time?"

The words were out before I could stop them. Next time. As if this wasn't a chance encounter, as if we did this regularly.

Carla's laughter faltered for just a moment, and I saw a flicker of something in her eyes. Uncertainty? Longing? Before I could decipher it, she recovered, her smile back in place.

"Deal," she said, and I tried to ignore the way my heart skipped at the prospect of seeing her again.

Carla took a sip of her coffee, her eyes meeting mine over the rim of her mug. "So, what about you? Any big plans for Thanksgiving?"

I leaned back in my chair, trying to maintain my casual demeanor. "Oh, you know, the usual Wells family extravaganza. Turkey, stuffing, and a healthy dose of awkward silence."

She tilted her head, curiosity sparking in her eyes. "Awkward silence? That doesn't sound like you."

I chuckled, but it felt hollow even to my own ears. "Yeah, well. It'll be different this year without Nathan and Rebecca there to run interference."

"Between you and your dad?" Carla asked softly.

I nodded, suddenly finding it hard to meet her gaze. I didn't want her to see how much the thought of my dad affected me. "Let's just say I'm not exactly looking forward to being the sole focus of Dad's... attention."

The words hung in the air between us, heavier than

I'd intended. I hadn't meant to let that slip, but something about Carla had always made it easy to be honest.

"Eli," she said, her voice gentle, "is everything okay?"

I swallowed hard, fighting the urge to brush it off with a joke. "It's just... you know how it is. Dad's always had these expectations, and I've never quite..." I trailed off, gesturing vaguely. My heart was tight in my chest at my admission. I never talked about this to anyone, so why was I spilling it now? This was far from the charming flirt I was trying to be.

Carla reached out, her hand hovering over mine for a moment before she seemed to think better of it. "You don't have to be Nathan, you know."

"Tell that to Dad," I muttered, then immediately regretted it. "Sorry, I shouldn't dump all this on you. It's not your problem."

But as I looked at Carla, I saw no judgment in her eyes, only understanding. I cleared my throat, desperate to lighten the mood. "Hey, speaking of Nathan, did I ever tell you about the time we decided to become circus performers?"

Carla's eyebrows shot up, a smile tugging at the corners of her mouth. "I don't believe you have. Do tell."

"We were, what, eight and ten? Nathan got it in his head that we could join the circus if we mastered some death-defying stunt." I leaned back in my chair, grinning at the memory. "So, naturally, we decided to practice tightrope walking."

"Oh no." Carla giggled, her eyes already sparkling with amusement.

"Oh yes. We strung up Mom's clothesline between two trees in the backyard. I went first, of course. Managed about three wobbly steps before I face-planted into Dad's prized rosebushes."

Carla burst out laughing, the sound warming something inside me I thought had long since gone cold. "Let me guess, Nathan chickened out?"

"Worse. Always the hero, he tried to 'save' me by jumping onto the line. We both ended up covered in thorns and Mom's unmentionables."

She was full-on belly laughing now, drawing curious glances from nearby tables. I found myself chuckling along, caught up in her infectious laughter.

"Your poor mother," Carla managed between giggles.

"Poor Dad's roses, more like. He was livid–at me, mostly." I shook my head, still smiling. "But Mom, bless her, she just patched us up and told us to try juggling next time. Less prickly landing."

As our laughter faded, a comfortable silence settled between us. It was far from the awkwardness of earlier, and I found myself reluctant to break it. Carla seemed to feel the same, her fingers idly tracing the rim of her now-empty coffee cup.

I watched her, allowing myself a moment to really look at her. The way the morning sun caught the highlights in her hair, the slight crinkle at the corner of her eyes from laughing. It hit me then how much I'd missed out on over the years. If we could have—

I couldn't go there. But I couldn't help wondering if she felt it too – this unexpected peace in each other's company.

"Elijah Wells, is that you?"

My stomach dropped as I turned to see Gladys Pinkman standing off to the side, scowling. I watched as her eyes darted between Carla and myself. "Good morning, Gladys," I said, without a hint of my usual warmth.

Her eyes widened as she gestured to the pair of us. "What do you think you're doing… with her," she hissed. "Your father would–"

Carla shrank back into her chair.

"My father," I ground out the words between clenched teeth, "would know that there is no harm in talking to an old friend."

Gladys gathered her shawl around her, scoffing her disbelief. "Well, we'll just see about that, won't we?" She stormed away.

I turned back to Carla, flashing an apologetic smile. "I'm sorry about that."

She sighed, twisting a strand of hair between her fingers. "It's fine. We should know better, right?" The short, cynical laugh sounded all wrong. She was hurt, and I wished I could make it better.

"I better head to the station," I said, reluctantly pushing my chair back. "Chief'll have my hide if I'm late again."

Carla looked up, a flicker of something—disappointment?—crossing her face before she masked it with a smile. "Can't keep Minden's finest from their duty, can we?"

I stood, draining the last of my definitely-not-pumpkin-spice latte. "Someone's gotta keep this town from burning down. Lord knows it's not gonna be my dad's attempt at deep-frying a turkey."

She snorted, shaking her head. "I'd pay good money to see that disaster."

"Tell you what," I said, surprising myself with my

next words, "how about I keep you posted on all the Wells family holiday shenanigans? You know, for old times' sake."

Carla's eyebrows shot up and she glanced toward Gladys's retreating frame. "Maybe that's not such a good idea."

"Oh." I shook myself out of the obvious daze I was in. "Yeah." She was right, of course. We were a bad idea. But every time I was with her, I couldn't seem to care.

I headed for the door, tossing a wave over my shoulder. "See you around, Putters."

She nodded sadly. "See ya."

As I stepped out into the crisp autumn air, the jingle of the cafe's bell seemed to echo the weird flutter in my chest. The encounter with Carla kept replaying in my mind—her laugh, the way she'd looked at me when I admitted my frou-frou coffee habit. And the way she'd retreated when confronted by Gladys.

This stupid feud would never stop haunting me, would it?

CHAPTER 4

Elijah

I wiped the sweat from my brow, grimacing as I finished polishing the last of the firefighter helmets. Nothing like some mindless grunt work to keep the hands busy and the mind quiet.

Jake yelled from across the station, "Your brother would be so proud—if he knew you actually worked once in a while."

I was filling in for Nathan's shift at the station today while he sipped some sort of pineapple drink on the beach. And I wasn't even exaggerating, because the jerk had actually sent me a selfie yesterday to gloat.

I shot him a mock glare. "Hey now, I'll have you know I'm employee of the month." I held up the gleaming helmet. "See? Sparkling."

The shrill ring of the emergency alert cut through our banter. We started moving toward the garage, even as we listened to the signal. The tone indicated it was a medical call. Then the dispatcher announced the address. The world tilted sideways.

I heard myself ask, "What happened?" but it sounded far away, like I was underwater.

That was my parents' address. The first address I'd ever memorized was just announced over the intercom at the fire station. My feet were moving before my brain caught up.

I sprinted for my locker, yanking on my jacket with shaking hands.

"I've got your back," Jake murmured. The concern in his eyes made my chest tighten further.

We raced for the ambulance and the truck, the usual excited chatter replaced by tense silence. I could feel the crew's sidelong glances, knew they were all thinking the same thing: poor Eli.

I clenched my jaw, willing the thoughts away. I had to focus on the job. That's all that mattered.

As we pulled out of the station, sirens wailing, I closed my eyes and sent up a silent prayer. Please let them be okay. Please let me be enough this time. Was it Linc? Or maybe Alex? I'd broken my arm when I was eight. Maybe it had been a mistake to let Mom and Dad take care of the kids. Or what if it was mom? They weren't ancient, but I'd seen crazier things happen. If one of the boys knocked her down the stairs by accident...

The fire truck's siren wailed as we tore through the streets of Minden, but it couldn't drown out the cacophony in my head. My knuckles were white on the seat's edge, my heart hammering against my ribs.

"The boys," I muttered, more to myself than anyone else. "God, I hope the boys are okay."

Jake's hand clapped my shoulder. "They're tough kids, Eli. Like their uncle."

I tried to smile, but it felt more like a grimace. "Yeah, well, being tough isn't always enough, is it?"

Images flashed through my mind—Alex screaming, Mom writhing in pain. I squeezed my eyes shut, willing the thoughts away. A hundred possible scenarios, fueled by the terrible accidents I'd seen as a first responder over the last eight years.

"Two minutes out," Jake called from the front. As we approached, the dispatcher fed us more information. Sixty-year-old male. Chest pain.

Not the boys, but it wasn't good. I sucked in a deep breath, steeling myself. As we rounded the corner onto my parents' street, I caught sight of their house. Nothing unusual. Just Mom's dried-out flower beds and Dad's perfectly manicured lawn. It looked so normal, it was surreal.

The truck screeched to a halt, and I was out before it fully stopped, my boots hitting the pavement hard. I sprinted up the familiar path, my heart in my throat.

"Mom!" I yelled, reaching for the door handle. It swung open before I could touch it, revealing my mother's tear-streaked face.

"Eli," she choked out, her voice trembling. "Oh, thank God you're here." She held one arm around Lincoln and the other around Joey. Alex stood back, his wide, dark eyes taking in the entire scene.

I pulled her into a quick, fierce hug, my eyes scanning the entryway behind her. "Where's Dad?"

I released her and held her at arm's length, searching her face. "What happened?" I asked, trying to keep my voice steady.

She drew a shaky breath. "We were just having breakfast, and he... he started clutching his chest." Her voice cracked. "He said it felt like a horse was sitting on him. I called 911 right away, but—"

"You did the right thing, Mom," I assured her, my protective instincts kicking in. I wanted to wrap her in my arms again, shield her from all this, but I knew I had to focus. "Where is he now?"

"Living room," she managed, pointing down the hall.

I nodded, squeezing her shoulder. "Okay, I'm going to check on him. The guys are right behind me with equipment."

As if on cue, Jake burst through the door, medical bag in hand. "Where to, Eli?"

"Living room," I replied, all business now. I strode down the hallway, my first responder training kicking in. "Dad?" I called out. "It's Eli. We're here to help."

I heard a weak groan in response, and my heart clenched. Rounding the corner, I saw him: my larger-than-life father, looking small and pale on the couch.

"Alright, Jake, let's get vitals," I ordered, my voice steady despite the turmoil inside. I could already tell we were going to transport him. His breathing was shallow and the pain was written across his face. "Matteo, get the stretcher."

The living room filled with the sounds of ripping Velcro and beeping monitors. I tried to focus on the task at hand, but my mind was working overtime in the background. This was my dad. The man who'd taught me to throw a baseball, who'd grilled me about my grades, who'd looked disappointed when I told him I was failing Physics.

"Eli," Dad's voice was barely above a whisper. "The boys..."

"They're fine, Dad," I assured him, even though I wasn't entirely sure. "Just focus on breathing, okay? We've got you."

"Matteo," I called out, "we're gonna need that stretcher in here ASAP. Jake, what's his BP looking like?"

I couldn't help but notice how fragile he seemed. It was unsettling, seeing him like this. Part of me wanted to crack a joke, lighten the mood somehow, but I knew this wasn't the time. Instead, I channeled all my energy into being the professional I'd trained to be.

I watched as Nathan's crew loaded Dad onto the stretcher, my heart pounding in my chest. The guys were being extra careful, treating him like he was made of glass. I wanted to tell them to hurry up, to get him to the hospital already, but I bit my tongue. They knew what they were doing.

"Eli, honey," Mom's voice quavered beside me. "What about the boys? I need to go with him." The indecision about what to do was tormenting her.

In all the chaos, I'd almost forgotten about my nephews. I ran a hand through my hair, my mind racing. "We'll figure something out, Mom. Don't worry."

But as I said it, I realized I had no idea what to do. Nathan and Rebecca were out of town, and most of our extended relatives lived hours away. Mom needed someone local, someone who could handle three rambunctious kids at a moment's notice.

And then it hit me. Carla.

My pulse skipped, a traitor to my composure. "I've got an idea," I told Mom, trying to sound more confident than I felt. "You go with Dad in the ambulance. I'll take care of the boys."

Her grip tightened on my arm. She didn't want to go without me either. I patted her arm. "I'll take them back to the station with me for now. When I get off shift, I'll meet you at the hospital, okay? It's just a few more hours." I glanced at my watch. Not even a few hours. The next shift might well be waiting for me when I got back to the station with the truck.

I could stay with the boys, but Mom needed me at the hospital. Thank God it was Saturday and Carla might actually be free.

I couldn't shake the feeling that I was about to

open a whole new can of worms. But what choice did I have? The boys needed someone, and Carla was the best option. Even if it meant stirring up old feelings and risking my dad's wrath.

I took a deep breath, bracing myself for what was to come.

I pulled out my phone, my thumb hovering over Carla's name. How many times had I almost called her, only to chicken out at the last second? I'd almost deleted her number a hundred times, but never had. Did she even still have the same number?

I hit 'call' before I could overthink it.

"Eli?" Carla's voice was a mix of surprise and wariness.

"Hey." I tried to keep my voice steady, but I could hear the strain in it. "Look, I know this is out of the blue, but I need a favor. It's... it's my dad. He's had a heart attack."

There was a sharp intake of breath on the other end. "Oh, Eli. I'm so sorry."

"Thanks. He's on his way to the hospital now, but..." I swallowed hard. "I need someone to watch the boys. I hate to ask, but—"

"Say no more," Carla interrupted. "I'll be right there."

Relief washed over me. "You're a lifesaver, Carla. Truly. Meet me at the station?"

Now I would just have to explain to Dad why the daughter of his sworn enemy was watching his grandkids. That'd go over well. One battle at a time, though.

I turned to see my crew loading up the truck. Mom was already in the ambulance with Dad, looking small and scared. I jogged over, squeezing her hand through the open door.

"It's going to be okay, Mom," I said, hoping I sounded more confident than I felt. "Someone's coming to watch the boys. I'll be there as soon as I can."

Mom nodded, her eyes glistening with unshed tears. "Thank you, sweetie. Your father... he'd be proud of how you're handling this."

I wanted to believe her, but doubt gnawed at me. Would Dad really be proud? Or would he be disappointed that I'd called Carla, of all people?

As the ambulance pulled away, its sirens piercing the quiet morning, I felt torn in a million directions. Part of me wanted to jump in my car and follow them to the hospital. Another part knew I had to go back to the station with the truck. And a tiny, traitorous part of me was actually looking forward to seeing Carla again.

Dad always did say I had my priorities mixed up.

"Is Papa gonna be alright?" Lincoln's curious voice made me turn.

I knelt down and opened my arms to the boys who'd stood silently by and watched us load their grandfather into the ambulance.

"The doctors are going to take a look at him and help him get better, okay?"

Three sets of trusting eyes looked back at me. Then three small nods of cautious acceptance.

"Why did Mimi leave? Is she sick too?"

I shook my head. "Mimi is just going to make sure Papa isn't scared. You guys are already so brave, she thought you'd be okay with it if she went with Papa instead. Is that alright with you? Are you my super brave boys?"

More emphatic nods this time.

"Since Mimi went with grandpa, you guys get to ride in the truck with me, okay? And then, Miss Carla is coming to hang out for a bit."

Smiles met the announcement, the first I'd seen from them since I arrived.

I strapped them in the best I could and climbed into the fire truck, my mind racing. *Please, God*, I prayed silently, *let Dad be okay. And maybe, while you're at it, don't let this whole Carla situation blow up in my face.*

Alex caught my eye in the rearview mirror. "I'm hungry. Can we get donuts?"

I chuckled. "Yeah, little man. We can definitely get donuts."

CHAPTER 5
Carla

My heart hammered in my chest, a staccato rhythm that matched the urgency of the situation. I'd never packed up and left the gym so quickly. I was still in my tank top and leggings. But the boys needed me, and I'd do anything for them. I loved them like they were my own family. I could be willing and still a little apprehensive, right? I'd babysat the boys before, but never in an emergency. I gripped the steering wheel, my knuckles turning white as I stared at the familiar brick facade of the fire station.

But the fact that Eli had called me for help? That made my heart a little shaky, too.

I muttered to myself as I stepped out of my car. "It's just Eli and the boys. No big deal."

Right. No big deal. Just the man who made my heart swoop in my stomach, like the drop of a roller coaster, every time I saw him, and three rambunctious kids I'd be responsible for. Piece of cake.

As I pushed open the heavy glass door, I was immediately welcomed into a homey scene. A handful of firefighters dotted the space. I recognized Kyle Parker and TJ Wolff, along with Jake and Matteo. The air was thick with the scent of diesel fuel and garlic, a combination that should have been unpleasant but instead felt oddly comforting.

My eyes scanned the room. I'd never been in the fire station before, but I was surprised to see it was set up sort of like a living room. I spotted a kitchen off to the left in the back, and several couches surrounded a large television.

My gaze immediately landed on Eli and the boys on the couch, Eli's dark hair and muscular frame unmistakable. He was in his uniform, the navy fabric stretched taut across his broad shoulders. My traitorous heart skipped a beat.

Another firefighter I didn't recognize was sitting down next to the boys, who were giggling as they focused on the video game on the big screen. The sight made me smile despite my nerves.

As if sensing my presence, Eli looked up. Our

eyes met across the room, and I felt that familiar jolt of electricity. His expression was a mix of relief and conflict, mirroring the turmoil I felt inside.

He started walking toward me, and I prepared myself for our interaction. How was I supposed to act around him? Professional? Friendly? Distant?

I watched Eli's broad shoulders tense as he approached, his firefighter uniform accentuating every muscle. My heart did that infuriating flip it always did around him, but I pushed the feeling aside. This wasn't about us.

"Hey," Eli said as he reached me, his voice low and gravelly. "Thanks for coming, Carla."

I nodded, trying to ignore the way my name sounded on his lips and the warmth that spread through my chest. "What's going on? Is your dad okay?"

He ran a hand through his dark hair, his eyes clouded with worry. "It's not good. He collapsed this morning. They think it is his heart. I need to get to the hospital, but..."

His gaze drifted to where his nephews were playing with a few of the other firefighters. I could see the conflict written all over his face.

"How are the boys doing?"

Eli ran a hand through his hair, a gesture I knew

meant he was stressed. "They're okay for now, but I'm worried about how they'll handle everything once it really sinks in."

I wanted to reach out and comfort him, but I held back. Instead, I said, "They're tough kids, Eli. We'll get through this together."

He raised an eyebrow at that, a hint of his usual cockiness seeping through. "We, huh?"

I felt my cheeks flush. "I just meant... All of us. Don't turn this into anything. This is about the boys and your father."

He nodded, his expression softening. "You're right. I'm sorry. I appreciate you being here, Carla. More than you know. I just..."

As I looked into his dark eyes, I could see the vulnerability he was trying so hard to hide. It made my heart ache, and I had to remind myself why I had kept my distance all these years. But standing here now, with Eli looking at me like that, all those reasons seemed to fade away.

"But you're worried about the boys," I finished for him.

"Yeah," he sighed. "I mean, I know they're in good hands with you, but..." I watched as Eli's jaw clenched, his eyes darting between me and the boys. His fingers drummed an anxious rhythm against his thigh, a tell I remembered all too well from our high school days.

"Look, I know this is a lot to ask," he said, his voice barely above a whisper. "And with our... history... I wouldn't blame you if you wanted to back out."

I fought the urge to roll my eyes. Classic Eli, always assuming the worst. "I'm here, aren't I?" I replied, trying to keep my tone light. "The boys will be fine. You need to focus on your dad."

Eli nodded, but I could see the hesitation in his eyes. He opened his mouth to speak, then closed it again, running a hand over his face.

"Spit it out, Wells," I prodded, crossing my arms. "What's really bothering you?"

He let out a shaky breath. "It's just... my dad. You know how he can be. If he found out you were watching the boys..."

I felt a twinge of hurt at his words, but I pushed it aside. This wasn't about me or our families' ridiculous feud. It was about those three little boys who needed someone to look after them.

"Your dad doesn't need to know," I said firmly. "Right now, all that matters is that you're there for him and your mom. Besides, I'm with the boys all the time. I've got this, Eli. Trust me."

Watching Eli's shoulders relax slightly, I knew I'd said the right thing.

"You're right," he admitted, his trademark grin finally making an appearance, though it didn't quite reach his eyes. "You always were the smart one, Puddles."

I rolled my eyes, but I couldn't help the small smile that tugged at my lips. "Someone has to be," I quipped. "Now, let's get these boys settled, shall we?"

We turned our attention to loading the kids into my sedan. As I helped buckle in the youngest one, I felt Eli's eyes on me. I pushed away the sudden awareness of my gym clothing. It was tight and hardly appropriate for the weather.

"Alright, munchkins," I said cheerfully, "who's ready for an adventure with Miss Carla?"

The boys cheered, their earlier hesitation seemingly forgotten. I couldn't help but grin at their enthusiasm. Teaching had its perks, and connecting with kids was definitely one of them.

Eli approached me as I closed the door, a folded piece of paper in his hand. "Here's my number and the garage code, in case you didn't have it. I'll be at the hospital, but I'll be back as soon as possible," he said, his voice low.

As he handed me the paper, our fingers brushed

ever so slightly. A jolt of electricity shot through me, and I saw Eli's eyes widen almost imperceptibly. For a moment, we were frozen, that brief touch speaking volumes about our unresolved history.

I cleared my throat, breaking the moment. "Got it. Don't worry, Eli. We'll be fine." I already have his number in my phone—I'd never been strong enough to delete it, and he called me no less than an hour ago—but his mind is clearly elsewhere.

As Eli drove off, I turned to the boys with a grin. "So, who's up for some fun?"

The older boy, Alex, eyed me skeptically. "What kind of fun?"

I tapped my chin, pretending to think hard. "Well, how about we start with building the world's biggest pillow fort?"

Their eyes lit up, and just like that, the ice was broken. I took them home, using the garage code to get into their house. We spent the morning constructing an elaborate fortress in the living room, complete with secret tunnels and a pillow drawbridge. As we worked, I kept my phone close, expecting updates from Eli.

Sure enough, it buzzed around noon.

Eli: Dad's stable. Tests ongoing. Thanks again for this.

I typed a quick reply, trying to ignore the flutter in my stomach at seeing his name on my screen.

Me: No problem. Boys are having a blast. Keep us posted.

Lincoln tugged at my sleeve. "Miss Carla, can we have dinosaur-shaped sandwiches for lunch?"

I grinned, pushing thoughts of Eli aside. "Absolutely! Let's see if we can make a whole Jurassic Park on our plates."

As we crafted our prehistoric lunch, my phone buzzed again.

Eli: You're a lifesaver. How are you managing?

I stared at the message, biting my lip. The genuine concern in his words made my heart do that annoying somersault again.

I snapped a photo of the dinosaur sandwiches and broccoli trees.

Me: We're good. I'm currently ruling over a kingdom of pillows and dinosaur sandwiches.

His reply came quickly.

Eli: All hail Queen Carla! May she always bless the kingdom with her beauty and grace.

I felt a warmth spread through me at the compliment, my cheeks blazing as I fought back the grin spreading across them.

Eli: Sounds like Dad's going to be okay. He's in

surgery now, and then it'll be medication and rest. He's probably here for 3-4 days at least, though.

Me: Wow. I'm glad he's okay.

I started typing a question, but deleted it. I didn't want to bother him while he was still dealing with everything. As long as someone was able to take the boys before I had to go back to school I would be fine. And since it was officially Thanksgiving break, we had a full week before that happened.

Before I could set down the phone, it began to ring in my hand. I glanced at the screen, seeing Eli's name flashing in bold letters. Swallowing my sudden nerves, I answered the call.

"Hey, Eli. Everything okay?" I tried to keep my tone light, masking the worry that threatened to seep in.

There was a brief pause on the other end before Eli's voice came through, gravelly with exhaustion. "We're all good here. Are you sure you're okay?"

My heart skipped a beat at the seriousness in his tone. "Of course. We're fine here." I hesitated. "Do you... do you know when you'll be back? Have you talked to Nathan or Becca?"

"I talked to Nathan and insisted they stay at the beach. Dad's going to be okay, and they deserve the break. Plus, their flights would be really expensive to change. Look, I hate to ask, but I won't be able to make it back tonight," he began, and I could hear the strain in his voice. "Mom needs me here, and I can't leave her alone."

My chest tightened with empathy for Eli and his family situation. "Don't worry about it," I replied without hesitation. "I'll take care of the boys for as long as you need. Can I give the boys an update, though? They're worried."

"Definitely. Tell them Grandpa's going to be okay. Actually... why don't you bring them to visit tomorrow? It'll be good for Dad to see them."

"Are you sure it won't be too much?" He assured me it wouldn't, and that he'd let me know if that changed.

After lunch the next day, I gathered the boys in the living room, my teacher voice kicking in. "Alright, team, we've got an important mission. We're going to visit Papa at the hospital."

Joey's little eyes widened. "Is Papa still sick?"

I nodded, keeping my tone gentle but firm. "He is, buddy. That's why we need to be on our best behavior. The hospital is a place where people go to get better, so we need to be quiet and respectful. Can you guys do that for me?"

Lincoln puffed out his chest. "I can be super quiet, Miss Carla. Like a ninja!"

I couldn't help but chuckle. "Excellent ninja skills will definitely come in handy. Now, let's get ready. Do you have those cards you made for your Papa?"

As the boys scampered off to fetch their hand-made creations, I took a deep breath. This visit was going to be tricky. I'd be lying if I said I wasn't nervous about potentially running into Harold Wells. The old feud between our families still cast a long shadow, and I wasn't sure how he'd react to seeing me there.

We piled into the minivan, the boys chattering excitedly in the backseat. After the twenty-minute drive to Greencastle, we pulled into the parking lot. "Okay, ninjas," I said, turning to face the boys, "remember our mission. Quiet and respectful, right?"

They nodded solemnly, and I felt a surge of affection for my best friend's kids.

As we made our way to the correct area, I spotted a familiar figure in the waiting room. Mrs. Wells sat in a chair, her face lined with worry. The moment she saw her grandsons, though, her expression brightened.

"There are my brave boys," she said, opening her arms.

Alex and Lincoln hesitated, glancing around at the unfamiliar environment. Then, as if a switch had been flipped, they rushed forward into their grandmother's embrace. Joey followed their lead, quickly scampering toward her.

"Mimi!" Lincoln exclaimed, then quickly lowered his voice to a stage whisper. "We're being quiet ninjas for Papa."

Mrs. Wells laughed softly, her eyes meeting mine over the boys' heads. I saw a flicker of surprise, then gratitude.

Alex pulled back, his face serious as only an eight-year-old can be. "We made cards for Papa," he announced, proudly holding up his colorful creation. "To help him feel better."

I watched as Mrs. Wells' eyes filled with tears. "Oh, sweethearts," she murmured, pulling them close again. "Papa will love these. They'll make him feel so much better."

As I stood there, watching this tender family moment, I felt like an intruder. But I also felt a warmth spreading through my chest. Despite everything – the family feud, the complicated history with Eli – I was glad I could be here for these boys.

Maybe some bridges were worth rebuilding, no matter how long they'd been broken. Could the bridge between our families ever be restored?

Just then, I caught a flicker of movement from the corner of my eye. My heart skipped a beat as Eli appeared, his firefighter's uniform replaced with a wrinkled T-shirt and jeans. His dark eyes met mine, a storm of emotions swirling in their depths.

"Uncle Eli!" the boys chorused, their faces lighting up.

Eli ruffled their hair, his smile not quite reaching his eyes. "Hey, kiddos. You being good for Carla?"

I nodded, trying to ignore the butterflies in my stomach. "They've been perfect gentlemen."

Eli's gaze locked with mine, a silent conversation passing between us. Gratitude, uncertainty, and something else I couldn't quite name flickered across his face. My breath caught in my throat.

"Boys," he said, breaking our eye contact, "want to go see Papa now?"

As they nodded eagerly, Eli turned to me with an apologetic smile. "Carla, I... uh, I think it might be best if..."

"If I wait here," I finished for him, forcing a smile. "No problem. I've got some emails to catch up on anyway."

Eli's shoulders sagged with relief, but I could see the conflict in his eyes. "Thanks," he murmured. "For everything."

As they walked away, I sank into a nearby chair, my mind a whirlwind of emotions. Part of me understood why I couldn't go in – Harold Wells' prejudice against my family was no secret. But another part of me felt a sharp sting of exclusion.

This wasn't about me. The man was in the hospital, for heaven's sake. I could sit in the corner and wait so he didn't get upset.

But as I sat there, surrounded by the hushed sounds of the waiting room, I couldn't shake the feeling that I would always be on the outside looking in.

CHAPTER 6
Elijah

I leaned against the doorframe, watching my nephews swarm around Papa's hospital bed like excited puppies. Alex, the oldest at eight, was showing off his LEGO shirt, while six-year-old Lincoln regaled Papa with a dramatic retelling of his favorite episode of Spiderman. Joey, not to be outdone, was attempting to climb onto the bed to get closer to the action.

"Easy there, buddy," I said, stepping forward to scoop up Joey before he could jostle any of Papa's tubes or wires. "Let's give Papa some breathing room, okay?"

As I settled Joey on my hip, I caught the tail end of the nurse's conversation with Mom. "...at least six weeks of rest and relaxation. No stress, no excitement. Just calm, quiet recovery time."

I suppressed a snort. Calm and quiet weren't exactly the Wells family's strong suits.

Mom's brow furrowed as she glanced from the nurse to the rowdy boys, then back to Papa. I could practically see the gears turning in her head as she tried to reconcile 'no stress' with 'three energetic grandsons.'

"We'll have to call Nathan and Rebecca," she said, wringing her hands. "They'll need to cut their trip short and come home early."

I felt a pang of guilt. Nathan and Rebecca needed this trip. They deserved some time to reconnect after walking through their rough patch this summer.

"No way, Mom," I said, shifting Joey to my other hip as he squirmed. "I can handle the boys. There's no need to ruin their vacation."

Mom's eyebrows shot up. "You? Eli, honey, I love you, but you can barely keep a houseplant alive. How do you expect to manage three young boys?"

I bristled at her lack of faith, even as a small voice in the back of my head whispered that she might have a point. But I pushed that doubt aside. "I think I can handle a few kids for a week."

As if on cue, Lincoln let out a war cry and launched himself at Alex, nearly knocking over the IV stand in the process.

"A week and a half," she corrected.

I winced. Okay, so maybe this wouldn't be a walk in the park. But I was determined to prove I could do this. To show Mom—and Dad—that I wasn't just the family screw-up.

"Look," I said, setting Joey down and corralling the other two before they could start World War III in the hospital room, "I know it won't be easy. But I can do this. Let Nathan and Rebecca enjoy their trip. I'll call them and make sure, but I've got this covered."

Mom still looked skeptical, but I could see her resolve wavering. I held my breath, waiting for her decision.

This was my chance to step up, to be the responsible son for once. And maybe to finally earn that look of pride from Dad that always seemed reserved for Nathan.

I met Mom's eyes, silently pleading. *Come on, Mom. Trust me. Let me do this.*

I held my breath as Mom's eyes darted between me and the boys, who were mostly quiet, coloring in the corner, making more cards for Papa. Finally, she let out a long sigh.

"Alright, Eli. You can watch them." The relief that washed over me was short-lived as she added, "But I'll be checking in every day."

"Thanks, Mom," I said, trying not to sound too eager. "I won't let you down."

I turned to share the news with Dad, only to find him eyeing me with that all-too-familiar look of doubt. It was like a punch to the gut, but I plastered on a smile anyway.

He grunted, adjusting his reading glasses. "This sounds like a recipe for disaster."

Ouch. I forced a chuckle, but inside, I was a mess of determination and anxiety.

As I herded the boys out of the room, Mom followed us. "Eli's going to be watching you for a while, boys. Be good for your uncle, okay?"

I caught Papa's skeptical snort as we left. Great. Nothing like a vote of confidence from dear old dad.

Back in the waiting room, I found Carla pacing, her dark hair swinging with each turn. When she saw me, relief flooded her face, quickly replaced by concern as she took in my expression.

"How's your dad?" she asked.

I ran a hand through my hair, suddenly feeling

the weight of everything crashing down on me. "He'll be okay, but he needs rest. A lot of it."

Carla's brow furrowed. "And the boys?"

"That's... complicated," I said, dropping into a chair. "I'm going to be watching them for a while."

Her eyes widened. "You?"

I let out a humorless laugh. Even Carla didn't think I could do it. "Mom's got her hands full with Dad, and well, Dad thinks I'm about as responsible as a circus clown on roller skates."

Carla's lips twitched, but she didn't smile. She knew me too well, could see the struggle behind my attempt at humor.

"Eli," she said softly, "are you sure about this? Three boys is a lot to handle."

I straightened up, pushing down the doubt that threatened to overwhelm me. "I can do this, Carla."

But even as I said it, I couldn't help wondering if I was in way over my head. Three energetic boys, a disapproving father, and ten days of chaos ahead. What could possibly go wrong?

I watched Carla's face as she processed my words. Her dark eyes flickered with uncertainty, and she bit her lower lip—a telltale sign of her inner conflict that I remembered all too well from our high school days. She shifted in her seat, her fingers absently playing with the hem of her shirt.

I pushed away the hurt that her hesitation caused. "I'm going to call Nathan and Rebecca and give them an update. Can you make sure these guys behave for a bit longer?" I pulled out my phone and made the call.

Nathan's face came across the screen. "Eli? How's Dad?"

"He's stable but needs rest. Which, as you could imagine, means the boys need a new plan."

I explained the situation, with Carla occasionally chiming in. Rebecca joined the call, her worry evident on her face.

"Are you sure about this, Eli?" Nathan asked, his tone cautious. "Three kids is a lot of responsibility."

"Maybe we should just come home," Rebecca said.

I felt a flash of irritation. "I'm not completely useless, you know. I can handle this."

Rebecca still seemed unsure. "I don't know…"

Seriously? I was so untrustworthy that she would consider canceling ten days in the Bahamas?

"Can I talk to Carla for a second?" Rebecca asked quietly.

I shrugged, handing the phone to Carla, who

quickly took the call to another corner of the room. I distracted myself with the boys so I wouldn't be tempted to eavesdrop.

A few minutes later, Carla came back. I raised an eyebrow with an unspoken question.

"Eli, Carla has agreed to help you take care of the boys for the rest of our trip," Rebecca said.

My mouth fell open. "What? That's really not–"

"Look, man," Nathan jumped in, "it's either this, or we come home. And I really don't want to come home yet," he admitted.

I ran a hand over my face. "Fine. So what? We'll trade off nights or something?"

Rebecca grinned. "You can all stay at our house. It'll be easier on the boys, and with both of you, it should be a breeze."

"Two adults are better than one when it comes to three rambunctious boys," Carla admitted.

I sighed. "Are you sure you're okay with this, Putters?" She hadn't exactly seemed thrilled when she came back from the sidebar with her bestie.

Carla nodded, but her expression was unreadable.

There was a pause, and I studied Nathan's expression. "We're trusting you, Eli."

My heart swelled hearing his words, before the

full truth hit me. He trusted me, as long as I had a chaperone.

His eyes darted slightly to the left, where I knew Carla would be shown on his screen. "Just… be careful, okay?"

I knew he wasn't just talking about the boys. He knew the history with Carla better than anyone. "We will, Nate. Don't worry."

As I hung up, I caught Carla's gaze. There was a mix of determination and something else in her eyes —something that made a twist of nerves coil tight in my belly.

"Well," I said, trying to lighten the mood, "looks like we're in for quite an adventure, huh?"

Carla took the boys home while I stayed at the hospital for a few more hours. Around five in the afternoon, I stepped into Nathan and Rebecca's house, immediately assaulted by a chorus of shouts and laughter. Three blurs – otherwise known as my nephews – zoomed past, nearly knocking me off my feet.

"Uncle Eli! We're starving!" Alex skidded to a stop in front of me.

I grinned, ruffling his hair. "Well, we can't have that, can we? What's on the menu, Chef Alex?"

"Pizza!" all three boys chorused.

I glanced at Carla, who was eyeing my duffle bag. "Pizza it is, then. Do you want me to call?"

Carla raised an eyebrow. "We're cooking instead. Rebecca keeps dough on hand. These hooligans can help. And you, I suppose."

I couldn't help but notice how her eyes lingered on my chest for a moment. Butterflies took flight in my stomach., but I pushed the feeling aside. *Focus, Wells.*

As we maneuvered around the kitchen, I found myself hyper-aware of Carla's presence. Every accidental brush of her arm sent tingles through me. I scolded myself. We weren't teenagers anymore.

"Alright, troops!" I called out, trying to wrangle the boys. "Who wants to be my official cheese sprinkler?"

Linc's hand shot up. "Me! Me!"

"Excellent choice, soldier. Alex, you're on sauce duty. And Joey," I said, addressing the youngest, "you're our very important pizza inspector. Make sure we don't miss any spots!"

Carla laughed, the sound warming me more than the preheating oven. "You're good with them," she said softly as she unrolled the refrigerated dough onto a sheet pan.

I shrugged, suddenly self-conscious. "They make it easy. They're great kids."

After what felt like hours of controlled chaos, we finally got the boys fed, bathed, and into bed. I collapsed onto the couch, exhausted but oddly satisfied.

Carla sank down on the other end of the couch. "We did it," she said, a note of triumph in her voice.

"Yeah, we did." I turned to look at her, struck by how beautiful she looked even with flour in her hair and tomato sauce on her shirt. I cleared my throat. "Uh, you should take the main bedroom. I'll crash on the couch."

She started to protest, but I held up a hand. "I insist. It's the least I can do after you agreed to help with this whole... situation."

Carla studied me for a heartbeat, her gaze softening. "You're not the same Eli I remember from high school, are you?"

I swallowed hard. "I'd like to think I've grown up a bit. Maybe even learned how to be responsible now and then."

She smiled, and I saw a flicker of the girl I'd fallen for all those years ago. "Good night, Eli," she said softly, standing up. My fingers ached with the urge to reach out and touch her. One thought of my dad lying in his hospital bed sent a twinge of guilt through me at my betrayal of his wishes.

This was going to be a very long week.

Ten days, I corrected with a grimace. I could handle ten days of essentially living with Carla. Then we'd just go back to our default setting of ignoring each other.

CHAPTER 7

Carla

I stepped out of the van, autumn leaves swirling around us due to the windy day. The boys exploded from the backseat like popcorn kernels, their laughter echoing across the park as they sprinted toward the playground.

"Whoa there, slow down!" I called after them, but it was no use. They were already scaling the jungle gym like tiny Spider-Men.

Eli chuckled beside me, his familiar cologne tickling my nose. "They've got more energy than a pack of Duracell bunnies."

I rolled my eyes, trying to ignore the way his smile made my stomach lurch, as if the ground had shifted beneath me. "Yeah, well, let's see how long that lasts. I give it an hour before someone's crying for a snack."

As we walked toward a nearby bench, I couldn't help but steal glances at Eli. His dark hair was tousled by the breeze, and his firefighter's physique was evident, even under his casual flannel shirt. I scolded myself. I was here to babysit, not ogle my high school ex.

"Earth to Carla," Eli's voice broke through my thoughts. "You okay? You look like you're solving world hunger in that head of yours."

I forced a laugh, hoping it didn't sound as strained as it felt. "Just thinking about the week ahead. Three boys, ten days... what could possibly go wrong?"

"Nine days," he corrected.

Nothing boosted a girl's ego more than knowing that he was counting down the minutes until we didn't have to share space anymore.

"Hey, we've got this," Eli said, bumping my shoulder playfully. "Between your organizational skills and my... uh, rugged charm, we're practically Mary Poppins."

I snorted. "Right, because nothing says 'magical nanny' like a small-town girl and a firefighter with a reputation."

The moment the words left my mouth, I regretted them. Eli's eyes darkened slightly, and I saw a flicker of hurt before his usual cocky grin slid back into place.

"Ouch, Puddles. Still got that sharp tongue, I see."

I took a deep breath, trying to center myself. This was exactly why I needed to keep things platonic. Every interaction with Eli felt like walking through an emotional minefield.

"Sorry," I muttered. "I didn't mean—"

"Forget it." Eli waved it off, but I could tell he hadn't. "Let's focus on making sure the rugrats don't start a *Lord of the Flies* situation over there."

As we settled onto the bench, I tried to shake off the memories flooding back—stolen kisses behind the bleachers, whispered promises, and the heartbreak that followed when our families found out. It felt like a lifetime ago, yet sitting there with Eli, it might as well have been yesterday.

I watched the boys play, their shrieks of joy filling the air, and reminded myself why I was there. This week wasn't about me and Eli. It was about being there for his family, for these kids who needed us. But as Eli's arm brushed against mine, sending shivers down my spine, I couldn't help but wonder if I was in way over my head.

I forced a laugh, trying to lighten the mood. "Well, at least they're burning off some energy. Maybe they'll actually sleep tonight."

Eli chuckled, his shoulders relaxing. "Dream on, Carla. I'm pretty sure these kids run on some kind of supernatural battery pack."

"Oh, come on," I teased, falling into our old rhythm despite myself. "The big, tough firefighter can't handle a few kids?"

He clutched his chest in mock offense. "Hey now, I'll have you know I can carry a full-grown man out of a burning building. But keeping up with three boys under ten? That's a whole different kind of endurance test."

I couldn't help but laugh, the sound mingling with his in a way that felt both familiar and dangerous. Why did everything with Eli have to feel so... easy?

"I don't know how you do it every day," he said, gesturing toward the playground. "Teaching a whole classroom of these little tornadoes."

I shrugged, a smile tugging at my lips. "It's not so bad. And middle schoolers are a different kind of challenge. More hormones. Less screaming, more attitude. At least I get to send them home at the end of the day."

"Unlike us this week," Eli added with a grin that made a tingle dance across my skin.

I was about to respond when Linc came barreling toward us, his face scrunched up in distress. "Aunt Carla! Uncle Eli!" he wailed. "I can't find my Spiderman!"

Eli was on his feet in an instant, his expression softening as he knelt to Linc's level. "Hey, buddy, don't worry. We'll find him. Where did you last see him?"

As Linc pointed toward the jungle gym, sniffling, I found myself rising to join the search party. Eli was already heading that way, his hand on Linc's shoulder, and I followed, trying to ignore the warmth blooming in my chest at his immediate willingness to help.

Why did he have to be so good with kids? It would have been so much easier to keep my distance if he was still the carefree, irresponsible boy I remembered. But this Eli, the one who dropped everything to find a lost toy? He was far more dangerous to my resolve.

I trailed behind them, watching as Eli began to scour the playground, his eyes darting from the slide to the sandbox. He was talking to Linc in a gentle voice, and I couldn't help but strain to hear their conversation.

"So," Eli said, peering under a bench, "who's your favorite superhero? Besides Spiderman, of course."

Linc's face scrunched up in thought. "Um... I like Iron Man too! He's super smart and builds cool stuff."

Eli chuckled, and the sound sent an unwelcome shiver down my spine. "Good choice. You know, when I was your age, I was all about Batman. I even made myself a cape out of one of my mom's old tablecloths."

I snorted at the mental image of a tiny Eli running around in a makeshift cape. He caught my eye and winked, causing my cheeks to heat up. I quickly looked away, focusing on searching the bottom of the slide.

"Did you get in trouble?" Linc asked, wide-eyed.

"Oh, big time," Eli admitted, grinning. "But it was worth it. I felt like I could take on the world in that cape."

As I watched Eli engage with Linc, my heart softened, despite my best efforts. This nurturing side of him was... unexpected. And annoyingly endearing. I found myself wondering what kind of father he might be someday, then immediately shut down that train of thought.

Suddenly, Eli let out a triumphant, "Aha!" and held up a small red-and-blue figure. "Look what I found hiding under the seesaw!"

Linc's face lit up like Christmas morning. "Spiderman!" he cried, rushing forward to claim the toy. Eli handed it over with a flourish, and Lincoln hugged it to his chest.

"What do we say, Linc?" I prompted gently.

"Thank you, Uncle Eli!" Lincoln beamed before darting off to show his brothers his recovered treasure.

"Nice work, superhero," I said to Eli, trying to keep my tone light, despite the dangerous softness creeping in.

He grinned that infuriating grin of his, then lowered his voice and tipped an imaginary hat with his fingers. "Just doing my duty, ma'am."

I rolled my eyes, but I couldn't quite suppress my smile. "Come on, let's get back to the boys before they decide to stage a jailbreak."

As we walked back to the bench, I found myself stealing glances at Eli, wondering how many more surprises this week had in store—and whether my heart could handle them.

Just as I was about to express my gratitude more sincerely, a jogger passed by, her ponytail swinging in perfect rhythm. She slowed her pace, flashing a dazzling smile at Eli and offering a flirtatious wave.

My heart plummeted as Eli returned the gesture with a friendly nod, his easy charm on full display. It was like watching a well-rehearsed dance, one I'd seen too many times before.

"Nice afternoon, isn't it?" Eli called out, his voice carrying that hint of playful warmth that seemed to draw women like moths to a flame.

The jogger's cheeks flushed, and she giggled —*actually giggled*—before continuing on her way, throwing one last glance over her shoulder.

I squashed the sudden wave of jealousy rising in my chest. This was classic Eli—the town's most eligible bachelor, leaving a trail of swooning women in his wake. It was exactly why I needed to keep my guard up.

"Friend of yours?" I asked, aiming for casual but landing somewhere closer to strained.

Eli shrugged, seemingly oblivious to the effect he had. "Nope. Just being neighborly."

I bit back a sarcastic retort, reminding myself that Eli's reputation wasn't my concern. Instead, I turned my attention back to the boys, watching them chase each other around the playground equipment.

"Hey, Alex!" I called out, forcing brightness into my voice. "Want to show me that new monkey bar trick you've been practicing?"

Alex raced over, excitement radiating from his face. I tried to focus on his chatter about hand positions and momentum. But a traitorous part of my mind kept replaying the jogger's smile and Eli's easy charm.

I knew better than to go down this road again. He was Eli Wells—charming, unreliable, and definitely not relationship material. I had to remember the heartache of him walking away. Remember why I was keeping my distance.

But even as I listed all the reasons to stay away, my heart whispered the counterarguments. The way he was with the boys. The familiar comfort of our banter. The way he seemed to let me see more of him than he showed anyone else.

I shook my head, pushing those thoughts aside. One week of forced proximity couldn't change years of history and family animosity. I plastered on a smile and focused on Alex's triumphant grin as he swung across the bars.

Suddenly, Eli was at my side, his presence

sending an unwelcome jolt through me. "Hey," he said, his voice low and warm. "The boys have been troopers today. What do you say we treat them to some ice cream?"

I glanced at him, surprised by the suggestion. It was thoughtful, and exactly the kind of distraction I needed. "That's actually a great idea," I replied, grateful for the chance to redirect my focus. I turned to the boys, raising my voice. "Boys! Who wants ice cream?"

Their excited cheers echoed across the playground as they raced toward us, faces lit up with joy. As we herded them toward the van, I couldn't help but smile. The drive to Dairy Freeze out by the interstate was mercifully short but long enough for Eli and me to fall into an unexpectedly comfortable rhythm. As he navigated the familiar streets of Minden toward the highway, I found myself relaxing despite my earlier resolve.

"Remember that time in high school," Eli said, a mischievous glint in his eye, "when we snuck out to get late-night sundaes and you dropped your entire cone in Nathan's freshly washed car?"

I groaned, the memory flooding back. "Oh, don't remind me. We both thought he was going to murder you."

"Hey, I was the perfect brother," Eli quipped. "Offered to lick it clean and everything."

I couldn't help but laugh, even as I rolled my eyes. As we traded more stories and jokes, punctuated by the boys' excited chatter from the backseat, I felt my guard slipping. It was so easy, so natural, to fall back into this pattern with Eli. The way he smiled when he teased, the way he didn't take himself too seriously.

But that small, protective voice in my head niggled at me. I couldn't get too comfortable. This was temporary. He hadn't changed.

I tried to heed that voice, anchoring myself in reality. Yet as Eli's laughter filled the truck, warm and genuine, it was like stepping into a memory—a time when things were simpler, and my heart wasn't weighed down by caution.

I had to stop. I had to focus on the kids.

Even so, when we pulled into the Dairy Freeze lot and Eli glanced at me with that familiar twinkle in his eyes, I knew I was fighting a losing battle.

The boys were practically vibrating with excitement. As we approached the ice cream counter, the sweet scent of sugar cones and vanilla wafted through the air.

"Alright, troops," Eli announced, clapping his hands together. "Who's ready for some ice cream?"

A chorus of enthusiastic cheers erupted from the boys. I couldn't help but smile at their unbridled joy.

"I want chocolate!" Alex declared confidently.

Linc nodded vigorously. "Me too! With sprinkles!"

Joey, however, looked overwhelmed by the colorful array of flavors displayed behind the glass. His little brow furrowed as he stood on his tiptoes, trying to get a better view.

Without missing a beat, Eli swooped in. "Here, buddy, let me help you out," he said, lifting Joey effortlessly onto his hip. "What looks good to you?"

As Eli patiently pointed out different flavors to Joey, explaining each one with animated descriptions, a warmth bloomed in my chest. It was a scene so achingly domestic, so natural, that for a second I let myself imagine what it would be like if things were different between us. If we weren't carrying the weight of our families' feud, if Eli wasn't... well, Eli.

I shook off the thought, focusing instead on helping Alex and Linc decide between toppings. But as I stole glances at Eli and Joey, I couldn't quite squash the longing that welled up inside me.

"What about you, Carla?" Eli's voice broke

through my reverie. "Still a mint chocolate chip girl?"

I blinked, surprised he remembered. "Uh, yeah. Old habits die hard, I guess."

He grinned, that heart-stopping smile I remembered all too well. "Some things never change."

And maybe some things could. That stubborn glimmer of hope flashed again, nestled in the center of my chest.

With our ice creams in hand, we settled at a nearby picnic table. The boys dove into their treats with gusto, their faces quickly becoming sticky messes of chocolate and sprinkles.

"So," Eli said, turning to the kids, "who's got the coolest superpower? Spider-Man or Superman?"

This launched an animated debate among the boys, each passionately defending their favorite hero. As they chattered away, I found my gaze drawn to Eli. He was listening intently to each child's argument, nodding seriously as if this were the most important discussion in the world.

Suddenly, he looked up, catching me mid-stare. Instead of the cocky smirk I expected, he offered a warm, genuine smile that sent my heart into overdrive. I quickly averted my eyes, focusing intently on my rapidly melting ice cream.

But even as I tried to find my resolve, I could feel my carefully constructed walls beginning to crumble.

The afternoon sun dipped lower, casting long shadows across the restaurant's outdoor seating area. I watched as the golden light caught Eli's profile, highlighting the strong line of his jaw and the crinkles around his eyes as he laughed at one of Joey's nonsensical jokes. My chest tightened with a familiar ache.

"Earth to Carla," Eli's voice cut through my thoughts. "You okay there? You're looking a little spaced out."

I forced a smile, hoping it didn't look as strained as it felt. "Just thinking about all the superhero homework I need to do to keep up with these guys."

Eli chuckled, his eyes twinkling. "Don't worry, I'll give you a crash course. Lesson one: capes are cool, but totally impractical."

The boys erupted into giggles, and I couldn't help but join in. As I watched Eli interact with them, I was struck by how natural he seemed, how effortlessly he had slipped into this role. It was a far cry from the reckless teenager I remembered.

"Alright, superheroes," I announced, standing up

and gathering our trash. "Time to head back to base. Your parents are planning to call tonight!"

As we walked to the car, Alex tugged on my sleeve. "Can we do this again tomorrow, Miss Carla? Please?"

I ruffled his hair, my heart swelling. "We'll see, buddy. One day at a time, okay?"

Eli caught my eye over the kids' heads, raising an eyebrow. "I like the sound of that... Sometimes, it's easier not to think about tomorrow. Or get hung up on the past."

I nodded, unable to formulate a response. As I helped buckle the boys into their seats, I took a deep breath. *One day at a time,* I repeated to myself. That's all I could handle right now. Whatever this thing with Eli was becoming, whatever this week might bring, I'd face it one day at a time.

CHAPTER 8
Elijah

I stepped out of Nathan and Rebecca's house, the crisp evening air nipping at my cheeks. It had been a relatively warm November, but it was still fall in Indiana. Ahead of me, my nephews zoomed down the sidewalk on their scooters, their laughter echoing through the quiet neighborhood. I couldn't help but grin, even as a twinge of anxiety hit my gut. Keeping up with those three was like trying to wrangle caffeinated squirrels. Carla and I had quickly discovered that exhausting them was the most reliable method of ensuring they didn't completely destroy the house–or each other.

"They're going to sleep well tonight," Carla commented beside me, a hint of amusement in her voice.

"If they don't, at least we will," I quipped, stealing a glance at her. The fading sunlight caught in her dark hair.

"You're good with them." Her casual words had my steps faltering.

"Careful, Putters. That sounded suspiciously like a compliment." Equally suspicious was the way my chest swelled with something like pride at her words.

I was rewarded with a shy smile, her face turning away from mine and back toward the boys, racing ahead of us.

"I should probably be honored, right? You're the expert, being a teacher and all that. I don't remember that being your plan... back then." What an eloquent way to reference our disastrous past. "What made you decide to pursue teaching?"

Her eyes light up, and I'm struck by how beautiful she looks when she's passionate about something. "Well, once I realized that being a professional cheerleader wasn't likely to work out..." She flashed a crooked smile, rolling her eyes as though laughing at her former self. Then, her voice warmed with enthusiasm. "I've always loved working with kids, and there's something magical about seeing that moment when a concept finally clicks for a student.

When I was a senior, I job shadowed Mrs. Lowell for a day. I thought I knew what a teacher did, but I only knew part of the story."

Mrs. Lowell had already been ancient when we were in elementary school. "Didn't she retire when we were in school?"

Carla nodded. "The summer after we graduated. But she still cared just as much as she always had that semester I shadowed her. It was pretty inspiring."

I was hanging on her every word. This was a far cry from the Carla I remembered from high school – still fiery and determined, but with a newfound depth that was even more captivating.

"Plus," she added with a mischievous grin, "I get to be the cool adult who knows all the latest TikTok dances."

I laughed, picturing Carla busting moves in front of a classroom of wide-eyed kids. "Now that I'd pay to see. Maybe professional cheerleader isn't too big of a stretch."

She rolled her eyes, but I caught the hint of a smile.

How different things might have been if my dad hadn't freaked out all those years ago. Would Carla and I be walking our own kids to the park instead of my brother's?

I pushed the thought away. No use dwelling on what-ifs, especially with the family feud still simmering beneath the surface. Instead, I focused on keeping an eye on the boys ahead, their scooters weaving dangerously close to each other.

"So," I said, desperate to keep the conversation going, "got any embarrassing student stories to share? I promise I won't tell a soul."

Carla arched an eyebrow. "Nice try, but teacher-student confidentiality is sacred. Unlike certain fire-fighters I know who love to brag about their heroic rescues."

"Hey, saving cats from trees is serious business," I protested, clutching my chest in mock offense. "I can't help it if Mrs. Solomon wants to tell the story to everyone in town."

She laughed, the sound warming me more than any fire ever could. And just like that, I was reminded of why keeping my distance from Carla Putnam had always been so difficult.

The crisp autumn air nipped at my cheeks as we strolled down the leaf-strewn sidewalk. With each step, leaves crunched beneath our feet, releasing that distinct earthy scent, triggering memories of bonfires and high school football games.

I was transported back to our high school days, sneaking glances at Carla across the classroom while pretending to pay attention to calculus.

"You really love it, don't you?" I asked, genuinely curious. "Teaching, I mean."

Carla sighed wistfully. "It's... amazing, Eli. Watching a kid finally grasp a concept they've been struggling with, seeing their confidence grow day by day. It's like... like being part of something bigger than yourself, you know?"

I nodded, understanding all too well. It sounded like the same pride I got after a call, knowing I made a difference. But there was something different about the way Carla described it, a warmth and passion that was uniquely her.

"There was this one student last year," she continued, her voice soft but filled with pride. "He was so shy, could barely look anyone in the eye. But by the end of the year, he was leading class discussions, helping other kids. That kind of transformation... that's why I do this."

Her face lit up as she talked about her students. I'd never really seen this side of Carla before, and I was struck with a twinge of regret for all the years we'd spent avoiding each other.

"Sounds like you're making quite the impact," I said, meaning every word. "Those kids are lucky to have you."

She glanced at me, a hint of surprise in her eyes. "Thanks, Eli. That... means a lot."

For a moment, we were both silent, the only sound the laughter of the boys ahead and the whisper of the wind through the trees. We were so close, it would be easy to reach out and take her hand. But I didn't. I couldn't. Instead, I shoved my hands in my pockets and focused on the path ahead, trying to ignore the way my heart raced every time she smiled.

The Carla I knew in high school was vivacious and fun. She cared about school and being popular. She was kind and far too smart to be with me. Nevertheless, my seventeen-year-old self was terribly convinced that she was perfect.

That girl was still there, but she was also someone strong, passionate, with a depth that was undeniably intriguing. The realization hit me like a punch to the gut: I'd missed out on watching her become this incredible person.

"You've really grown," I blurted out before I could

stop myself. "I mean, not like, physically grown. Well, you have, but—" I stumbled over my words, as if I'd been body snatched by an awkward teenager. "What I'm trying to say is, you're an impressive woman."

She raised an eyebrow at me, a mix of amusement and skepticism on her face. "Impressive, huh? High praise from the town hero."

I winced internally at her words. If she only knew how far from a hero I felt most days. "I'm serious," I insisted. "The way you talk about your students, your dedication... it's admirable."

A small smile played at the corners of her mouth. What I wouldn't give to see it more often. "Well, thanks. You're not so bad yourself, Eli. When you're not being a complete pain, that is."

I chuckled, but there was a heaviness in my chest. How different would things be if I hadn't pushed her away all those years ago? If I'd been brave enough to stand up to my dad?

A gust of wind whipped through the trees, and Carla shivered, wrapping her arms around herself. Without thinking, I shrugged off my jacket and held it out to her. "Here, take this."

She looked at the jacket, then at me, surprise evident in her eyes. "Oh, I couldn't—"

"Come on, Putters. I'm not gonna let you freeze out here. What kind of gentleman would that make me?"

She snorted. "Since when are you a gentleman?"

"Ouch." I placed a hand over my heart in mock hurt. Entirely imaginary. Definitely not offended that she considered me a... What did she consider me?

"What's the opposite of a gentleman?" I pondered out loud.

Her hand flew to her mouth to cover a sharp laugh. "What?"

"Well, if I'm not a gentleman, what am I? A cad?"

She tapped her chin with a finger, and my eyes caught on the red polished fingernail. "A boor, perhaps?"

"A bore? Surely not. I'm far too interesting to be a bore."

I held out the jacket again, and this time Carla hesitated only briefly before reaching for it. Our fingers brushed as she took it, and I swore a jolt of electricity shot through me. It was ridiculous how such a small touch could affect me, but I couldn't deny the way my heart started racing.

"A *boor*," she corrected, drawing out the word like she was savoring it. The jacket swallowed her petite frame, and I couldn't help but think how adorable she looked in the oversize garment.

"You know, rude, uncultured, eats with his mouth open. That kind of thing."

I smirked, slipping my hands into my pockets as the chill nipped at my now jacketless arms. "Well, I do chew with my mouth closed, so maybe we can strike that one off the list."

She tilted her head, pretending to think. "Fine. Not a boor. But definitely not a gentleman either. What about... a rake?"

My grin faltered for a fraction of a second before I leaned into it, keeping the edges sharp. "A rake, huh? Charming, dangerous, irresistible? I mean, I'll take it."

"Rakes aren't exactly known for their good intentions," she pointed out, her eyes gleaming with challenge. "It's more like charming, dangerous, *irresponsible*."

"Semantics." I waved her off like it didn't sting more than I cared to admit. "Besides, you're still standing here warm and toasty while I am jacket-free, freezing to death. Dangerous? Sure. But irresponsible? Case closed."

"Bold of you to assume I haven't been carefully weighing my escape routes," she teased, but the faint blush in her cheeks betrayed her. Probably the cold. Definitely the cold.

I leaned a little closer, letting my voice drop conspiratorially. "You don't want to run. Admit it. Rakes are way more interesting than gentlemen."

Her laugh was immediate and bright, breaking through the frost in the air. "I'll give you interesting. But if you're a rake, what does that make me? The lowly, unsuspecting governess who falls for your questionable charms?"

"Sounds about right." I gave her a wink, but the word *lowly* lodged itself somewhere uncomfortable. My father might see her as beneath us, but truthfully, she was far superior. "Except you're way too smart for that."

"Oh, absolutely." She raised an eyebrow. "I'm not falling for anything."

That made two of us. Not falling into anything.

"Which brings us back to square one," I said with mock seriousness. "If not a rake or a boor or a cad, then what? A clown?"

That did it. She doubled over with laughter, clutching her sides. "Oh no. You can't put that out there. You're one-hundred-percent a clown."

"Whoa, whoa, whoa," I said, holding up my hands as if I'd just been accused of something truly heinous. "Clowns are terrifying. And not in the charming, dangerous way. More like the nightmare fuel way."

She wiped at her eyes, still giggling. "What's the difference?"

"Seriously? *Seriously?*" I leaned back, feigning shock. "Have you seen my shoes? Perfectly normal size. No squeaky noses here, Putters."

"No, but you do have the jokes. And the inability to take anything seriously." Her smile softened, and so did her voice. "You're kind of clown-adjacent, whether you like it or not."

"Adjacent, huh?" I muttered, rubbing the back of my neck. "I can work with that. Adjacent leaves room for improvement."

"Oh? Is that what we're doing here? Improving you?" Her lips quirked up, but there was a flicker of something warmer behind her teasing.

"Hey, you're the one trying to pin a label on me," I shot back, cocking an eyebrow. "Rake, clown, boor— it's exhausting trying to live up to your expectations."

"I never said they were high expectations."

The words hit like a punchline, sharp and precise. But the look she gave me—half-challenging, half-inviting—kept me from retreating behind the wall I'd perfected.

I flashed her a grin that I didn't quite feel. "That's probably wise of you," I said, a self-deprecating joke drawing an end to the exchange.

The moment passed, but her laughter lingered in the air, softer now, like an echo that refused to fade. I should've shrugged it off—the teasing, the labels, the way she didn't quite let me take myself too seriously. That's what I was good at, after all. Laugh it off, throw in a joke, deflect before anyone could get close enough to see the cracks. But Carla? She had a knack for getting past the jokes, for poking at the places I didn't want to acknowledge, even to myself.

And blast it all, I cared. More than I should. Her opinion shouldn't matter. It couldn't matter. But when she looked at me, I felt this stupid, aching need to prove something. To be something more than the clown, the rake, the guy who didn't take anything seriously. I hated how much I wanted her to see me differently—how much I wanted her to see me at all. It wasn't just about the labels she tossed at me like darts; it was about the warmth behind her words, the flicker of understanding in her eyes when she wasn't trying to make me laugh. That scared me more than any joke ever could. Because if she was right—if I was more than the masks I wore—what did that make me? And worse, what would she think if she ever saw the man underneath?

Our loop around the block completed, we arrived back at Nathan and Rebecca's house a minute after the boys. A whirlwind of activity hit us as soon as we stepped through the door. The boys are bouncing off the walls, still hyped up from their scooter adventure.

"Alright, munchkins," I announced, clapping my hands. "Who's ready for the world's most epic bedtime routine?"

Carla shot me an amused look.

I put on my best game show host voice. "Step right up, ladies and gentlemen, for the Wells-Putnam Bedtime Extravaganza!"

To my surprise, Carla jumped right in. "First event: The Lightning-Fast Tooth Brushing Challenge!"

We tag-teamed the boys through brushing, pajamas, and a quick bedtime story. It was chaotic, but there was a strange comfort in the mayhem. It felt natural, working with Carla, the five of us like some kind of... family.

Whoa. Pump the brakes, Wells.

After we finally got the boys settled, I collapsed

dramatically onto the couch. "Wake me up when Rebecca and Nathan get home." Never mind that it would still be six more days.

Carla chuckled, patting my leg. "Still think you're hot stuff, Mr. Firefighter?"

Me, hot? No. Except where her hand was resting on my calf. That was scorching.

"I'll take a four-alarm fire over bedtime any day," I joked, but there's a part of me that wasn't entirely sure I didn't mean it.

CHAPTER 9

Carla

I leaned against the porch railing, soaking in the laughter that filled the yard. My eyes were drawn to little Joey, his chubby legs pumping furiously as he pedaled his miniature bike across the driveway. His face was the picture of pure, unadulterated joy – the kind only a two-year-old could muster on a sunny afternoon, even with a stocking cap tugged over his ears to ward off the chill.

"Careful there, speed racer!" I called out, more out of habit than any real concern. After all, what could possibly go wrong on such a perfect day?

The universe, apparently eager to prove me wrong, chose that exact moment to intervene. Joey's front wheel hit a crack in the drive, where the concrete had settled an inch or so. It was just enough to send him toppling sideways. Time seemed to slow as I watched him fall, his laughter morphing into a startled cry.

My heart leaped into my throat, and before I knew it, I was sprinting across the yard. My instincts kicked in, pushing aside the panic that threatened to overwhelm me. I dropped to my knees beside Joey, my hands hovering over him as I quickly scanned for any serious injuries.

"Hey there, buddy," I said, keeping my voice steady despite the adrenaline coursing through me. "That was quite a tumble, huh? Can you look at me?"

Joey's bottom lip quivered, his eyes wide with shock as he wailed, pointing to his knee. The kid could talk nonstop, but apparently words were too much work when he was crying.

I glanced down, my stomach clenching at the sight of blood through a hole in his sweatpants.. *A lot* of blood. Just what we needed to round out this babysitting adventure – an actual injury. But even as the sarcastic thought flitted through my mind, I pushed it aside.

"It's okay, sweetie," I soothed, gently brushing his hair back from his forehead. "We'll get you fixed up in no time. Can you be my brave little monkey for a minute?"

At the mention of his favorite animal, Joey's crying lessened. His face brightened slightly. "Ooh ooh, ahh ahh!" he mimicked, hiccupping through his tears.

I couldn't help but chuckle, marveling at how quickly children could bounce back. "That's right, just like a brave little monkey. Now, let's see what we can do about that knee, shall we?"

As I reached for Joey's leg, a shadow fell over us. I looked up, my breath catching in my throat as I recognized the broad-shouldered silhouette. I braced myself for the inevitable flip-flop of my traitorous heart as Eli crouched down beside us.

I watched as Eli's expression shifted from his usual playful smirk to a look of focused concern. His dark eyes scanned Joey's injury with a calm I couldn't seem to muster, and I felt an unwanted twinge of admiration. I hated how good he was at this. Why did he always have to show up at moments like this? And why, oh why, did he have to look so infuriatingly competent while doing it?

"Hey there, little man," Eli said, his voice warm and steady. "Mind if I take a look at that knee?"

As he spoke, my mind raced with thoughts of how to handle the situation. Should I take Joey to the emergency room? Was a first-aid kit enough? And why did Eli's presence have to complicate everything?

Joey nodded bravely, but I saw the fear still lingering in his eyes. I found myself holding my breath as Eli gently examined the wound, his touch so careful, so... capable. "It's a deep scrape, but nothing too serious," Eli said, glancing up at me. "We just need to clean it and bandage it up."

"I can handle this," I muttered, more to myself than to him. "I've dealt with worse scrapes before."

Eli raised an eyebrow, that trademark cockiness starting to creep back into his expression. "I'm sure you have, Carla. But two pairs of hands are better than one, don't you think?"

I gritted my teeth, trying not to let his words get to me. But he was right—of course, he was. I couldn't do it alone, not with Joey sobbing like that and my own nerves about to unravel.

When I returned with the first-aid kit, I knelt beside Eli again and let myself watch him. He was so focused, so good at what he did. Irresponsible? No. Careless? My chest tightened, the memories of our past—of what he'd done to me, of how he'd hurt me —flooding back. No, that wasn't this guy.

As Eli opened the kit and began cleaning Joey's wound, I turned my attention to the little boy's tear-streaked face. His bottom lip quivered, threatening a fresh bout of tears.

"Hey, Joey," I said softly, brushing his hair back from his forehead. "Did I ever tell you about the time I fell off my bike and thought I'd turned into a superhero?"

Joey's eyes widened, momentarily distracted from the sting of antiseptic. "Really?"

I nodded, launching into an embellished tale of my childhood mishap. As I spoke, I watched Eli out of the corner of my eye. His hands moved with practiced efficiency, cleaning the cut with gentle precision.

"...and that's why I thought I could fly for a whole week," I finished, earning a giggle from Joey.

Eli chimed in, his voice light. "Well, if anyone could pull off being a secret superhero, it'd be Miss Carla here."

I cleared my throat, suddenly aware of how close Eli and I were sitting. "Good job, buddy," I said to Joey, ruffling his hair. "You were so brave."

Eli nodded in agreement. "Tougher than some of the guys at the fire station, that's for sure."

As Joey beamed at the praise, I caught Eli's eye. I looked away quickly, my mind a whirlwind of conflicting emotions. This unexpected teamwork was dangerous territory, and I wasn't sure I was ready to navigate it just yet.

As Eli carried Joey toward the porch, I trailed behind, my mind reeling.

"You coming, Carla?" Eli called over his shoulder, that familiar smirk playing at the corners of his mouth. "Or are you just enjoying the view back there?"

I rolled my eyes, grateful for the chance to slip back into our usual banter. "In your dreams, Wells," I shot back, quickening my pace to catch up. I had most definitely not been enjoying the view. Even if his jeans were slightly dusty from where his shoes had pressed into his back pockets. I didn't notice at all.

As we settled onto the porch, Joey curled up contentedly in Eli's lap, I found myself stealing glances at the pair of them. Eli's strong arms cradled Joey protectively, his usual cockiness replaced by a gentle tenderness that made my heart do somersaults.

I caught myself staring at Eli's profile, noticing the way his dark hair curled slightly at the nape of his neck, how his brow furrowed with concentration as he gently adjusted Joey in his lap. This wasn't the cocky, devil-may-care Eli I was used to deflecting.

This was... someone else. Someone I found myself wanting to know better.

"You know," I said suddenly, my voice almost too quiet, "I always thought your whole firefighter gig was just another way to show off. But seeing you in action today... I get it now."

Eli's gaze flicked toward me, a teasing grin tugging at the corners of his mouth. "Oh? Do tell, Miss Putnam. What exactly do you 'get'?"

I rolled my eyes, trying to push down the fluttering in my chest. "That maybe there's more to Elijah Wells than meets the eye."

He paused, his playful expression shifting. For a split second, I thought I saw something flicker—something almost vulnerable—in his eyes. But then it was gone, replaced by that cocky smirk I was far too familiar with.

"Careful there," he warned, "you're dangerously close to giving me a compliment again."

My heart skipped a beat. That wasn't the point, but I couldn't ignore the way my body was reacting to him. I wasn't stupid. I knew the score. I knew the kind of man Eli was—he'd never stick around, never choose me, not when his family's legacy was involved. He had his own world, one I didn't fit into.

So why, in this moment, did I want so badly to

just lean into the warmth between us? Why did my heart keep betraying me, reminding me of what could never be?

I looked away quickly, forcing a casual tone back into my voice. "Don't let it go to your head," I said, trying to make it sound light. But even I could hear the softness in my words, and that terrified me. I couldn't let myself care. Not again. He was a playboy, irresponsible, someone who never let anyone get too close. I knew firsthand that he would never choose me over his family—over the life he had built around those old grudges. And yet, here I was, practically clinging to the warmth of his gaze.

For a moment, I allowed myself to imagine what it would be like if things were different. If we weren't caught between feuding families and years of carefully constructed walls.

But just for a moment. Because reality couldn't be avoided.

JOEY, Linc, and Alex were already full of excitement before we even left the house. I had to remind them a dozen times to behave, to stop chasing each other, and to hold my hand when we crossed the street. It was always like this, a whirl-wind of noise and motion. Joey and Lincoln were always in constant motion, and Alex—well, he was still young enough to not think before he ran off if he saw a squirrel or something interesting in the distance.

It was easier with Eli, but he was working today. By the time we reached the library, I was nearly winded, but I managed a smile. The library looked like something straight out of a storybook. The red brick building sat nestled between an old antique shop and a small office building that had been empty for years. It wasn't anything fancy, but it had that comforting, homey feel. Its front door was heavy, and the boys fought over pushing the automatic opener button.

The bell above the door chimed softly as we stepped inside, and the musty scent of books washed over me, filling my lungs with nostalgia. It was a smell that always made me think of summer after-noons spent curled up with a good novel, the sun streaming in through the windows.

Samantha was behind the desk, sorting through a pile of books. Her daughter, Sophia, was sitting at one of the tables in the corner, reading her own book. Sophia was thirteen, but I didn't have her in my class at school.

Samantha glanced up when the door chimed, her lips curving into a friendly smile. She was always warm and inviting. Today, her calm demeanor was a perfect contrast to the chaos the boys brought into the library. She was dressed in a cozy sweater and jeans, and her hair was tied up in a messy bun. I often wondered how she managed to juggle being a single mom and a full-time librarian. From the outside, she always seemed to have everything under control. But I knew better than to assume it was as easy as it looked.

"Hey, Carla!" she called over. "How are you today?"

I smiled back, my heart lifting at the sight of her. "Good, good. Just trying to wear the boys out before we head home. And maybe sneak in a little reading time myself."

Samantha chuckled, and I could see her eyes crinkling with amusement. "I get that. I heard you were watching Rebecca and Nathan's boys while they were gone. With that handsome brother of his. Elijah, right?"

I waved a hand, trying to keep the heat from rising in my cheeks. "Eli is working a lot. I'm happy to help," I said, desperately hoping for a change of topic.

"Shame about Mr. Wells's heart attack, isn't it? Have you heard how he is?"

I forced a tight smile. Okay, was it too much to ask for a *different* change of topic? "He's coming home the day after tomorrow, I believe."

"That's good. It's really nice of you to watch these hooligans. What's on the agenda today?"

"Books, hopefully," I said, practically sighing with relief and giving Joey a pointed look as he was already racing toward the shelves of the children's area. "But you know how it goes with them. They'll probably end up running circles around the place. I'll try to keep them quiet."

"Don't worry about it too much," Samantha said, winking. "I can't blame them. If I were their age, I'd want to burn off some energy too. And it's practically a ghost town in here this week. They won't bother anyone."

I nodded, glancing over at Sophia. "She's a good one," I commented. She was completely absorbed in whatever book she was reading.

Samantha followed my gaze and smiled. "Yeah, she really is." Her tone was wistful, almost sad.

I'd often noticed an especially deep bond

between Samantha and her daughter—something special and strong. It made me wonder how much Samantha really had to go through to raise Sophia on her own. The town knew next to nothing about Sophia's father, and I could never help but wonder what his story was. Samantha had always been so tight-lipped about it, and I respected her privacy, but I'd be lying if I said I wasn't curious.

I didn't pry, of course. That wouldn't have been right. But it was hard not to notice that, while Samantha had a lot of friends in town, she often seemed like she was keeping people at arm's length. I couldn't imagine how hard it must have been for her to raise Sophia without the support of a partner, especially in a small town like this where everyone knew everyone else's business.

"Boys," I called out, grabbing their attention, "let's take a look at the new books. I want you all to pick something."

Joey was already rifling through a stack of board books, pulling them out of the bin and tossing them aside like he was looking for buried treasure. Linc, on the other hand, was fascinated by the animal encyclopedias. He loved learning about different species, his curiosity unending.

About twenty minutes later, and a hundred

reshelved books, I wrangled all the boys. "Alright, boys, time to head out," I called, clapping my hands together. The library's quiet atmosphere had been a nice change of pace, but I knew the boys wouldn't last much longer without creating some chaos.

Joey and Lincoln raced toward me, and I ushered them toward the door, giving Samantha a final wave. "Thanks for having us, Samantha. We'll see you soon."

"You're always welcome, Carla," she called after me, her voice warm and genuine. "Take care."

As we left the library and the boys started their usual running-around routine, I felt a small pang of something in my chest. There was a quiet strength to Samantha that I longed for—something I wished I could carry with me when times got tough.

Maybe I wouldn't be letting Eli's presence this week send me into such a tailspin. Samantha sure seemed like nothing rattled her.

CHAPTER 10

Elijah

I paused at the threshold of Room 302, my hand hovering over the door handle. The antiseptic smell of the hospital corridor burned my nostrils, reminding me of countless emergency runs. But this time, I wasn't here to deliver a stranger. I was here to face my father.

Taking a deep breath, I squared my shoulders and pushed open the door. The sight of Dad propped up in bed hit me like a punch to the gut. He looked better than he had a couple days ago, but that wasn't saying much. His skin was still ashen against the crisp white sheets, and the usual larger-than-life presence I associated with Harold Wells had shrunken considerably.

But as his eyes met mine, I saw that familiar stubborn glint. Some things never changed.

"Hey, old man," I said, plastering on my best easygoing grin. "Looks like they're treating you pretty well in here."

Papa's eyebrows furrowed, but I caught the ghost of a smile tugging at the corner of his mouth. "Eli. They let just anyone in here?"

As I settled into the chair, I couldn't help but think how surreal this was. The great Harold Wells, looking so... mortal. It was like seeing Superman laid low by kryptonite. I'd spent so much of my life trying to measure up to this man, and now here he was, looking frail and vulnerable.

But those eyes – those eyes were the same as always. Watching me, assessing me, waiting to see if I'd finally do something to make him proud. I'd have thought he would have learned not to hold his breath.

I cleared my throat, pushing away the heavy thoughts. "So, how's the food here? Up to your gourmet standards?"

Dad snorted. "If by 'gourmet' you mean 'bland mush,' then sure. I'd kill for one of your mother's pot roasts right about now."

"I'll sneak you in some contraband next time." I

winked, but my heart wasn't in the joke. There was an elephant in the room, and its name was Carla Putnam. But after the last several days, I couldn't pretend anymore. I needed to understand.

I took a deep breath, bracing myself. "Listen, Dad... there's something I wanted to ask you about." I paused, searching for the right words. "This whole thing with the Putnams... don't you think it's time to let it go?"

The change was instant. Dad's face hardened, his jaw clenching tight. "There's nothing to discuss about that family," he said, his voice flat and cold.

I leaned forward, frustration bubbling up inside me. "Come on. It's been years. Whatever happened between you and Jim Putnam—"

"I said, there's nothing to discuss," Dad cut me off, his eyes flashing with a familiar stubbornness. He turned his head away, staring out the window.

I sighed, running a hand through my hair. This was going about as well as I'd expected. But I couldn't just let it go. Not when Carla's smile haunted my dreams, not when the thought of her made my heart race like I was facing down a five-alarm fire.

"Dad, please," I tried again, my voice softer this

time. "I'm not asking for details. I just... I need to understand."

The silence stretched between us, thick and heavy. I watched his profile, the stubborn set of his jaw, the way his fingers twisted the thin hospital blanket. My mind raced, searching for the right words to break through his defenses.

"Look," I said, leaning in closer, "I know this isn't easy to talk about. But don't you think it's time? I mean, we're not getting any younger here." I attempted a chuckle, but it fell flat. "And let's face it, Dad, your ticker's given us all a scare. Don't you want to clear the air before—"

"Before what?" Dad snapped, his eyes finally meeting mine. "Before I kick the bucket? Is that what you're saying, Eli?"

I winced. "No, that's not— I just meant—"

"I know exactly what you meant," he growled. "And let me tell you something. What happened between me and Jim Putnam doesn't concern you or anyone else in this town."

I felt my own temper rising, matching his. "Doesn't concern me? Dad, it's affected our whole family for years! And now—" I cut myself off, Carla's face flashing in my mind.

His eyes narrowed. "And now what? This isn't

about some misguided crush on that Putnam girl, is it?"

My cheeks burned. "It's not a crush," I muttered, feeling like a teenager again. "Carla and I... we have a connection. And maybe if we could just move past this ridiculous feud—"

"Ridiculous?" Dad's voice was low and dangerous. "You have no idea what you're talking about."

I stood up, pacing the small room. "That's the point. You won't even tell me why I'm supposed to hate them." My mind was a whirlwind of conflicting emotions—frustration with Dad's stubbornness, longing for Carla, and the ever-present desire to make my father proud.

How could I choose between my family and the woman who made my heart race? The thought of angering Dad twisted my gut, but the idea of letting Carla slip away again was equally painful.

The silence that fell between us was thick enough to cut with a knife. I stared out the window, watching a flock of birds swoop past, wishing I could fly away from this whole mess. My shoulders sagged, the weight of unspoken words pressing down on me.

I let my guard drop. "Dad," I said softly, my voice barely above a whisper, "I just want to understand."

Dad's gruff voice cut through the air like a thunderclap, showing his ire despite his weakened state. "The Putnams are nothing but trouble, Eli. Always have been, always will be. Jim Putnam is a snake in the grass, a chip off the old block, and that girl of his is cut from the same cloth. And I want you to keep her away from those boys."

I whirled around, frustration and determination warring inside me. "You don't even know her! Carla's not—"

"Elijah Joseph Wells," Mom's voice rang out from the doorway, startling us both. "I could hear you two hollering halfway down the hall. What on earth is going on in here?"

I glanced at Dad, seeing the fire in his eyes dim slightly at Mama's presence. He cleared his throat. "Nothing, dear. Just a little father-son chat."

"Some chat," I muttered, but I felt my own anger deflating.

Mom bustled into the room, her no-nonsense energy filling the space. "Well, whatever it is, it stops now. Harold, you need your rest, and Eli, don't you have to get home to the boys?"

I nodded, grateful for the excuse to escape. "Yeah, I should get going."

As I moved toward the door, Dad's voice stopped

me. "Eli," he said, his tone still hard, "don't push me on this. Some things are better left in the past."

I didn't turn around. "Bye, Dad. Get some rest."

I stepped out into the hallway, my mind spinning like a tornado. Carla's face flashed before my eyes, her dark hair framing that mischievous smile I couldn't seem to shake. What a mess. Here I was, thirty years old, feeling like a teenager sneaking around behind my old man's back.

I leaned against the wall, closing my eyes for a beat. What if getting involved with Carla would only lead to heartache? But then I remembered the warmth of her hand in mine, the spark in her eyes when we talked. It felt real. More real than anything I'd felt in years.

One thing was for sure – I wasn't ready to give up on Carla without a fight. I'd just have to make my father understand somehow.

THE FRIDGE CAST a faint glow across the dark kitchen as I stood there, debating whether midnight pickles were a craving or a cry for help. I'd been up for hours, despite my exhaustion, reliving every conversation, every interaction. No matter how tired I was, I couldn't shut them off. Regret, guilt, confusion—they all swirled together, like I was trapped in a loop of my own making.

I needed something, anything, to stop the noise in my head. Something simple, something stupid like pickles. But deep down, I knew it was more than that. It was me, trying to hold onto control in a situation that felt like it was slipping through my fingers. Torturing myself with the mistakes of my past and the shackles of the present.

I couldn't move forward with Carla, not with my father's disapproval. But every conversation with her made it harder to stay in this strange limbo. He was coming home tomorrow, and our conversation at the hospital earlier had been a disaster.

Deciding it was too late to try and philosophize my way through the mess in my mind, I reached up for the top shelf, my movements automatic, and began rummaging around.

"Midnight snack raid?"

I turned to find Carla leaning against the doorway, looking adorably rumpled in oversized pajamas that slid off one shoulder. Her hair was a mess, dark strands tumbling loose around her face, and a faint crease from her pillow marred her cheek. She was entirely too close, entirely too comfortable. As though my chaotic thoughts had summoned a vision to torment me further.

"Guilty as charged," I admitted, holding up a jar of pickles as if that explained everything. "Care to join me in my delinquency?"

She rolled her eyes, but there was a tug at the corner of her lips as she slid onto a stool at the kitchen island. "You and your weird pickle obsession. I swear, you haven't changed a bit."

"Oh, I've changed," I say, trying to keep the lightness in my tone. "I can reach the top shelf now, for starters."

Carla snorted, a sound that should be unflattering but somehow wasn't. "Congratulations. What other incredible feats have you mastered?"

I hesitated, the air between us shifting as I weighed my next words. "I'd like to think I've learned a thing or two about mistakes. The hardest part isn't making them—it's living with the knowledge that you didn't have to."

I clenched my jaw, mentally scolding myself for taking the conversation there. It'd been casual, meaningless midnight chatter. But I just had to go and say something deeper. As though anyone expected deep thoughts from me.

Her lips parted slightly, and for a moment, she

simply looked at me. The room felt smaller, the dim light casting her face in soft shadows. The sound of her breathing, slow and steady, felt loud in the quiet.

She reached out and snagged a pickle from my plate, her fingers brushing mine in the briefest, electric touch that I tried not to let affect me. Finally, she spoke, her voice gentle but firm. "You can't undo the past, Eli. But you can learn from it. I think that's all any of us can do."

I blinked, taken aback by the simplicity of her words, the calmness in her tone. It was the kind of truth I didn't want to hear but needed. She wasn't offering sympathy, just honesty.

I could feel the weight of her gaze still lingering on me, but instead of the usual distance between us, there was something different—something fragile. Maybe even hopeful.

I let out a quiet breath, my fingers tightening around the jar. "Guess I've still got a lot to learn then."

Her lips curved slightly, not quite a smile but something close. "We all do."

And just like that, the moment passed. She took another bite of the pickle, as if we hadn't just crossed some unspoken line.

But I felt it, deep in my chest. I'd let her see a

little beyond the rake or the clown, and she hadn't laughed in my face or belittled my experience. She'd understood. And that was even more dangerous than the swath of bare shoulder playing peekaboo behind the tendrils of her hair as I watched her head back to the bedroom. I settled onto the couch, my mind finally calming enough to doze off.

I woke with a start, heart pounding. The darkness outside was still thick, but the first hints of light were starting to creep through the windows. The shriek echoed through the house—sharp, high-pitched, and full of terror. Carla.

My body reacted before my mind could catch up. I shot off the couch, adrenaline flooding my veins as my instincts kicked in. The sound of my bare feet slapping against the hardwood floor echoed in the quiet house, every step a blur of urgency. I passed the empty bedroom, a knot tightening in my gut. She wasn't there.

I skidded to a halt in front of the master bathroom door, my fist already raised, pounding against the wood.

"Carla!" My voice was rough with panic. "Are you okay? What's happening?"

The scream had quieted. Outside, the world was still half-dark, as though it, too, was holding its breath. The silence of the house was deafening, broken only by the frantic pulse of my heart and the faint, eerie hum of the coming dawn.

My mind raced through a dozen worst-case scenarios. Did someone break in? Was she hurt? The protective surge I felt caught me off guard, but I pushed the realization aside, focusing on the immediate crisis.

"I'm coming in!" I shouted, ready to break down the door if necessary.

Just as I was about to throw my shoulder against it, the door flew open. Carla stood there, dripping wet and clutching a towel around herself. Her eyes were wide, cheeks flushed.

"Eli! I'm so sorry, I didn't mean to wake you," she said, breathless.

I blinked, confusion replacing my panic. "What happened? Are you hurt?"

She shook her head, droplets of water flying from her dark hair. "No, no. It's just... in the shower. I may have overreacted a bit. But in my defense, that spider could take down a small child."

Relief washed over me, quickly followed by embarrassment at my dramatic response to her distress. I tried to steady my breath. "Do you want me to take a look?" I offered, but part of me prayed she'd already smashed it. I hated spiders.

"Would you? That'd be great," Carla said, stepping back to let me into the room.

Blast. Okay, I could do this. I was a firefighter, for crying out loud. I walked into burning buildings. I could handle a spider. I briefly considered putting my gear on, and it was just out in my truck. But that would be ridiculous.

I followed her into the bathroom, but everything about the space felt too close. The scent of her shampoo lingered in the steamy air. Carla pulled back the shower curtain, and I froze. Her proximity was overwhelming, every inch of the small space suddenly charged with something neither of us was willing to acknowledge.

Our eyes met, and for a second, the room felt like it shrunk even further. I forgot to breathe. The tension between us was so thick, it practically crackled.

I swallowed hard, the knot in my throat stubborn, and forced myself to look at the spider instead of her. She wasn't making it easy, though. My heart squeezed with something else I couldn't quite place. Desire? Maybe. But I refused to go there, to admit what this was. I should have stepped back, given her space, but my body refused to cooperate.

She pointed to the ceiling, and I jumped at the sight of the spider in the corner. It was the size of my watch. Of course, it was.

I searched for a weapon, my pulse spiking. Nothing. I darted into Nathan's closet, grabbing a shoe as if it was going to save me from the impending doom of a eight-legged monster.

I took a deep breath, grabbing a wad of toilet paper to dispose of the nightmare. I could do this. I could. In one of the last conversations I had with Nathan, he kept going on about slaying dragons for his wife. Maybe this counted.

After a moment of terror, when I thought it might escape, I tossed the evidence of the gruesome murder into the trash can. I ran a hand over my rumpled hair and turned to look at Carla, sure to keep my eyes firmly focused on her eyes. "All set."

Carla tightened her grip on her towel, eyes searching mine. "Thanks, I appreciate it."

"No problem. All part of the service, ma'am."

She rolled her eyes at my attempt at humor, but her lips twitched with the hint of a smile. It was enough to undo me. I should leave, but the pull of her presence is a heavy weight, keeping me rooted to the spot.

The air between us was thick with unspoken words, with every glance lingering just a fraction too long. As I turned to leave, I couldn't help but wonder how much longer we could keep pretending there was nothing between us.

I forced myself to move, but stopped in the doorway, my hand resting on the frame. I didn't look at her. "Hey, Carla?"

"Yeah?"

"Try not to wake the whole house next time, okay? Some of us need our beauty sleep."

She laughed, the sound warming me more than any shower could. It shouldn't affect me this much, but it did. "Get out of here, Wells."

As I closed the door behind me, I leaned against it, eyes shuttered. Living this close to Carla was going to be the death of me. But what a way to go.

CHAPTER 11

Carla

I sat in the stillness of my car, my hands resting in my lap as my thoughts churned. My conversations with Eli kept replaying in my mind—his teasing, his quiet vulnerability, the way his eyes seemed to ask questions I wasn't ready to answer. It wasn't supposed to be like this. I wasn't supposed to feel like a teenager again, torn between loyalty to my family and the pull of someone who made my heart race.

What was I doing? It was just supposed to be a couple of days of helping out, nothing more. But now, every time I closed my eyes, it was Eli's smile I saw, his laugh I heard.

A decade ago, it had been Eli who walked away. I hadn't understood at the time. I was oblivious, happily head-over-heels for him. Until he shut me out and never explained why. It wasn't until later that I'd heard the truth. Eli's father had forbidden him from seeing me. And he'd obeyed.

I didn't blame him. Truly, I didn't. We were kids. It was puppy love, right? But that didn't mean it hadn't hurt. It still hurt to think about. I couldn't blame him for choosing his family over me. But I would be lying if I didn't wish he'd chosen differently. Or at least... handled it differently? Would it have hurt less if he'd been honest about it? I wasn't sure.

What I did know was that I didn't want to live in the shadow of old grudges. I wanted to live in the present, and the present, right now, was calling me to Eli.

I could already feel the tension that would greet me when I walked into my parents' house. It was inevitable. Dad wouldn't like what I had to say, but I had to say it. I couldn't let fear of his anger dictate my life anymore. I had to face him.

Taking a deep breath, I squared my shoulders and walked toward the door. It was time. Time to lay everything out and finally tell my father that I was my own person—one who was starting to think for myself, starting to make choices for reasons other than family loyalty.

I stepped into my parents' living room, the familiar scent of the fire mingling with Mom's lemon-scented furniture polish. Dad sat in his worn leather armchair, paper rustling as he turned the pages of his John Grisham novel. My heart thumped against my ribs as I took a deep breath, readying myself for the conversation ahead.

"Hey, Dad," I said, trying to keep my voice casual as I sank onto the plush floral couch. "How's the book?"

He grunted noncommittally, eyes still skimming the chapter. I fidgeted with a throw pillow, gathering my courage.

"So, uh, I had an interesting week," I ventured. "I'm babysitting the Wells boys for a few days."

Dad's head snapped up, his bushy eyebrows furrowing. *Oh boy, here we go.*

"The Wells boys?" he echoed, shutting his book with a crisp snap. "What in tarnation are you doing with them?"

I shrugged, aiming for nonchalance. "Harold and Patty were supposed to watch them while Nathan and Rebecca took a trip, but Harold had a heart attack."

Dad snorted, but I ignored it. "So, Rebecca needed help. You know me, always happy to lend a hand."

Dad's face darkened like storm clouds rolling in over the Blue Ridge Mountains. I braced myself, wishing I could melt into the couch cushions and disappear.

"Carla Jean," he began, his tone carrying a warning, "I thought we'd been clear about associating with those people."

Those people. As if the Wells family were some kind of alien species instead of our neighbors for the past three generations. I bit back a sarcastic retort, reminding myself that antagonizing Dad wouldn't help my case.

"Come on, Dad," I said, keeping my voice light. "They're just kids. It's not like I was plotting some kind of Wells-Putnam alliance."

Even as the words left my mouth, I felt a twinge of guilt. Because while I might not have been plotting anything, the time I'd spent with Eli had definitely stirred up feelings I thought I'd buried long ago.

Dad's frown deepened, creating canyons in his weathered face. "It's not about the kids, Carla. It's about principles. About loyalty to your family."

I resisted the urge to roll my eyes. Sometimes, I wondered if Dad realized we were living in the 21st century, not feudal Scotland.

"I am loyal to my family," I insisted, sitting up straighter. "But that doesn't mean I have to ignore half the town because of some ancient grudge."

The moment the words left my mouth, I knew I'd pushed too far. Dad's face flushed red, a vein throbbing in his temple. I braced myself for the impending lecture, wishing I'd kept my big mouth shut.

"Ancient grudge?" Dad's voice rose, his hands gripping the armrests of his chair. "Is that what you think this is?"

I tucked a stray lock of hair behind my ear, trying to calm the nervous energy coursing through me. "Dad, I—"

"No, you listen here, young lady," he cut me off, leaning forward. "Have you forgotten what that family did to us? To your grandfather's business?"

I felt my jaw clench, the familiar knot in my stomach tightening. Of course I hadn't forgotten. How could I, when it was brought up at every family gathering, every holiday dinner? Eli's grandfather and my grandfather had been business partners. Until Eli's grandfather torpedoed the business. No one knew why. Or if they did, they weren't telling me. That was the most frustrating part. No matter how much I pushed, I never got the whole story.

"Whatever happened—whatever the reason was? That was decades ago," I said, struggling to keep my voice steady. "And his kids had nothing to do with it. You and Harold used to be friends, didn't you?

Dad scoffed, his eyes narrowing. "The apple doesn't fall far from the tree, Carla. You're being naive."

I bit my lip, memories of Eli's kind smile and gentle teasing flashing through my mind. If only Dad knew how wrong he was. But I couldn't tell him that without revealing too much.

"I'm not naive," I argued, my frustration building. "I'm just trying to live my life without being weighed down by ancient history."

Dad's voice boomed, making me flinch. "Your Grandpa Kenny lost everything. And you think that's ancient history?"

I closed my eyes for a moment, willing myself to stay calm. When I opened them, I met Dad's gaze head-on. "I understand why you're upset, but—"

"No, you clearly don't," he interrupted, his face flushed with anger. "If you did, you wouldn't be fraternizing with the enemy."

The word 'enemy' echoed in my head, and I couldn't help but think of Eli's warm laugh, the way his eyes crinkled when he smiled. Some enemy.

"They're not the enemy, Dad," I said softly, my heart heavy with the weight of unspoken truths. "They're just people, like us."

Just as I thought Dad might explode, Mom's gentle voice cut through the tension like a cool breeze on a sweltering day.

"Jim, honey," she said, placing a hand on his arm, "maybe we should all take a deep breath. Carla's a grown woman now, and she's always had good judgment."

I shot Mom a grateful look, feeling some of the tightness in my chest ease. Dad's shoulders relaxed slightly, and I seized the moment to gather my thoughts.

"Look," I began, taking a deep breath, "I know this is complicated, and I understand why you're worried. But I'm not a little girl anymore. I can make my own decisions."

Dad opened his mouth to argue, but I held up a hand. "Please, let me finish. I'm not trying to hurt you or disrespect our family's history. But I can't live my life based on a feud that started before I was born."

As I spoke, I couldn't help but think of Eli. His cocky grin, his quick wit, the way he always seemed to know just what to say to make me laugh. But there was more to him than that – I'd seen the vulnerability in his eyes when he talked about trying to prove himself to his father.

"The Wells boys aren't their father or grandfather," I continued, my voice steady despite the butterflies in my stomach. "They're just... people. Good people, actually. And Eli, he's..." I trailed off, realizing I'd said more than I meant to.

Dad's eyebrows shot up. "Eli? The troublemaker? Don't tell me you're getting involved with him again."

I felt my cheeks flush. "That's not what I meant. I'm just saying, they're not the villains you think they are. And I need you to trust me on this."

As the words left my mouth, I realized how true they were. I did need Dad to trust me, because the truth was, I wasn't even sure I trusted myself when it came to Eli Wells.

Dad's face hardened, his disappointment etched in the deep lines around his eyes.

I stood up, my legs trembling slightly. "I'm not going to abandon my friends or treat them differently because of something that happened decades ago."

The air in the room felt thick, heavy with unspoken words and lingering resentment. I could feel Dad's disapproval radiating off him in waves, but I refused to back down. My heart raced as I grabbed my purse, desperate to escape the suffocating atmosphere.

"I should get going," I said, my voice barely above a whisper. "I'll see you later."

As I walked out, I couldn't shake the knot of unease in my stomach. Why did everything have to be so complicated?

Five minutes later, I pulled into Nathan and Rebecca's driveway, the tension in my shoulders easing slightly at the sight of their cozy two-story house. The porch light was on, casting a warm glow over the front yard where the boys' bikes lay scattered.

I took a deep breath, trying to shake off the remnants of my argument with Dad. As I approached the front door, I felt a smile tugging at my lips despite myself.

I opened the door, and there he was, sprawled on the couch, flipping through channels with a bored expression. A fire department T-shirt clung to his muscular frame, and I forced myself not to stare.

"Hey, stranger," I said, plopping down next to him.

Eli's face lit up with a grin that never failed to make me feel warm all over. "Well, if it isn't my partner in crime. The boys are asleep. Did you have a good time at Bible study?"

I shrugged. "It was fine. What are we watching?"

He must have sensed something in my voice because his expression softened. "You okay, Carla? You seem a little... off."

"Just family stuff. I stopped by my parents' after small group," I said, waving a hand dismissively. "Nothing a good distraction won't fix."

Eli's eyes twinkled mischievously. "Distraction, huh? I think I can manage that." He flipped to a channel playing reruns of *Friends* and turned to me with a triumphant grin. "How's this for a blast from the past?"

As the familiar theme song filled the room, I felt a wave of nostalgia wash over me. "Perfect," I admitted, settling back into the cushions.

"So," Eli said, his voice teasing, "on a scale of one to 'I'm rubber, you're glue,' how mature was this family drama?"

I snorted, nearly choking on my water. "Let's just say my dad's still firmly in the 'Wells family bad, fire hot, stars pretty' camp." I gave my best caveman impression with the words.

"Ah, the classics," Eli nodded sagely. "And here I thought my boyish charm would have won him over by now."

"I don't think there is any risk of you winning him over anytime soon," I retorted, but I couldn't help the smile that spread across my face.

As we watched, trading quips and laughing at the on-screen antics, I found myself relaxing more and more. It was dangerous, this easy camaraderie with Eli. I knew I should keep my distance, but in moments like these, it was hard to remember why.

"You know," Eli said during a commercial break, his voice softer now, "whatever's going on with your family... I'm here to listen or distract you or what-ever you need. Anytime. You know that, right?"

I looked at him, surprised by the sincerity in his dark eyes. For a few seconds, I allowed myself to imagine what it would be like if things were differ-ent, if there wasn't this invisible wall between us.

"I know," I said quietly. "Thanks, Eli."

He bumped his shoulder against mine playfully, breaking the moment. "Anytime, teach. Now, important question: Ross and Rachel—were they on a break?"

I groaned, throwing a pillow at his head. "Don't even start!"

I leaned back against the side of the couch, feeling a sense of peace wash over me that I hadn't experienced in ages. The tension from my earlier conversation with Dad slowly melted away, replaced by the comforting presence of Eli and the familiar sitcom hijinks playing out on screen.

As our laughter filled the room, I realized that for the first time all day, I felt truly at peace. And if a small part of me wished this moment could last forever? Well, that was a problem for another day.

Without warning, Eli reached over and pulled my feet into his lap. I tensed for a moment, ready to pull away, but then I caught sight of his profile—jaw clenched slightly as he focused on the TV, trying to act casual. Oh, great. Cue the heart gymnastics.

I should have moved. I really should have. But... maybe just this once, I could let myself enjoy the moment without overthinking it.

"Comfortable?" Eli asked, his tone light but with an undercurrent I couldn't quite place.

"Mmm," I mumbled noncommittally, refusing to

give him the satisfaction. "Your lap makes a passable footrest, I suppose."

He snorted. Then he began to knead the balls of my feet, and I bit back a groan. My eyes fell closed, and I listened to the dialogue and the laugh track as he slowly eased the tension from my body. This was playing with fire. But the heat felt so good.

As the episode drew to a close, I found myself stealing glances at Eli. The way the light from the TV played across his features, highlighting those dark eyes that always seemed to see right through me.

When the credits finally rolled, I turned to face him fully, surprised by the softness I found in his expression.

"Hey," I said quietly. "Thanks for the distraction. I really needed it tonight."

A familiar smirk tugged at the corner of Eli's mouth. "What can I say? Providing quality entertainment is just another of my many talents. Right up there with dashing good looks and exceptional firefighting skills." He winked. "And unbeatable foot massages."

I rolled my eyes but couldn't help the laugh that escaped. "And don't forget that stunning modesty of yours."

But even as the teasing words left my mouth, I noticed something in Eli's eyes. A warmth, a sincerity that made my breath catch. For a moment, the cocky firefighter facade slipped away, revealing the boy I'd known all those years ago.

"Anytime, Carla," he said softly. "I mean it."

And despite all my reservations, despite the voice in my head screaming about feuding families and playboy reputations, I found myself believing him.

CHAPTER 12

Elijah

I wiped the same spot on the fire truck's gleaming red hood for the tenth time, my mind a million miles away from the task at hand. The rag moved in mindless circles as I replayed my latest encounter with Carla. Her dark eyes had flashed with that familiar mix of annoyance and something else—something that made my heart try to surge out of my chest.

I was so lost in thought, I didn't hear Chief Danny approach until he cleared his throat. I nearly jumped out of my skin, whirling around to see him standing there with an amused smirk on his face.

"Trying to rub a hole in that truck, Wells?" He gestured to the spot I'd been scrubbing relentlessly.

I glanced down at the rag in my hand, realizing

I'd been polishing the same spot for who knows how long. *Smooth move, Eli.* I plastered on my trademark grin, hoping to cover my embarrassment.

"Just making sure it's extra shiny, Chief. You know, in case Matteo needs to check his hair on a call."

The Chief's eyebrows shot up and an amused smile crossed his lips.

"I heard that!" Matteo called from across the truck bay. I laughed, grateful for the easy banter.

"Just being prepared," I called back.

"Speaking of being prepared," Danny said, leaning against the truck, "you seem a bit... distracted today. Everything alright?"

I felt my smile falter for a split second before I caught myself. "Who, me? Nah, I'm good. Just, uh, pondering the great mysteries of life. You know, like why hot dogs come in packs of ten but buns only come in packs of eight. That kind of thing."

Chief raised an eyebrow, clearly not buying it. "Uh-huh. And I suppose these 'great mysteries' have nothing to do with a certain dark-haired school-teacher?"

I froze, a nervous excitement curling in my belly. Was I that obvious? "I don't know what you're talking about," I said, trying to keep my voice casual.

"But, hypothetically speaking, what if a guy found himself in a situation where he, I don't know, had feelings for someone he probably shouldn't?"

Chief Danny's expression softened. "Hypothetically, huh?"

I nodded, suddenly finding the fire truck's gleaming surface fascinating. "Yeah, you know, asking for a friend."

"Well," the chief said slowly, "I'd tell your 'friend' that matters of the heart are rarely simple. Especially in a town as small as Minden."

I couldn't help but snort. "You got that right. It's like trying to keep a secret in a town where everyone has a porch and a pair of binoculars. Hypothetically, of course."

The chief leaned against the fire truck, his weathered face creasing with a knowing smile. "Eli, let me tell you something I've learned over the years. Life's too short to let other people's opinions dictate your happiness. If there's someone who makes your heart race, someone who challenges you to be better, you owe it to yourself to explore that."

I felt my chest tighten at his words. The chief's calm demeanor and understanding tone made me want to spill everything, but I held back, my usual defenses kicking in. "Even if it might cause, I don't know, a small-town civil war?"

"Especially then," he said, his voice firm but kind. "The people who truly care about you will come around. And those who don't? Well, their opinions aren't worth sacrificing your chance at happiness."

I paused in my work, the rag hanging limply from my hand as I absorbed his words. My mind inevitably drifted to Carla—her quick wit, her infectious laugh, the way her eyes lit up when she talked about her students. A warmth spread through my chest, quickly followed by a familiar twist of anxiety.

Could I handle it if Dad never came around?

"But what if—" I started, then stopped, swallowing hard. The second reason I hadn't pursued Carla had pushed to the forefront of my mind. "What if you're not good enough for them? What if you're just the family screw-up and everyone knows it?" I stared at the rag in my hands, fighting back the burning sensation in my eyes.

The chief's hand landed on my shoulder, solid and reassuring. "Elijah, that's your father's voice talking, not yours. And not the Lord's. You're a darn good firefighter and an even better man. Don't let anyone tell you different. Even him."

I nodded shakily, a lump forming in my throat.

The chief's words echoed in my head, battling against years of doubt and insecurity. "I don't know if I can risk it," I admitted.

The chief watched me, his weathered face softening. His voice took on that sage-like quality that always made me feel like a kid in Sunday school. "Life's too short to let fear call the shots. Sometimes, you've got to be willing to risk it all for what really matters." He clapped me on the shoulder and hummed as he walked away, presumably to offer life advice to another poor firefighter.

As I turned back to the task at hand, my mind was racing. Maybe it was time to stop running, to face this head-on. The idea terrified me, but there was an undercurrent of excitement too. What if I actually had a shot at happiness?

I scrubbed at a particularly stubborn spot on the truck, my movements mirroring the determination building inside me. Maybe it was time to be bold, to take a risk.

I paused mid-scrub, the soapy sponge dripping onto my boots. "What if it all goes up in flames, Chief?" I asked his retreating back, unable to keep the hint of vulnerability from creeping into my voice. "And I don't mean the kind we can put out with a hose."

He chuckled, the sound warm and reassuring. "Then you pick yourself up, dust off the ashes, and keep moving forward. That's what we do, isn't it?"

I nodded, a small smile tugging at the corners of my mouth. The chief had a point. We faced down danger every day. How much scarier could it be to face my own heart?

I blew out a breath. At least a thousand times scarier. I was pretty sure that was a good estimate.

CHAPTER 13
Carla

I stepped onto the porch, the cool evening air a welcome reprieve from the chaos inside. The boys had finally settled down, but their energy still buzzed through my veins like a lingering sugar rush. Above me, fairy lights twinkled, casting a soft glow that seemed to smooth the rough edges of my doubts.

Leaning against the porch railing, I let out a long breath. The wood was sturdy beneath my hands, grounding me in the moment. My mind drifted, replaying the day's events – laughter, spills, and the constant juggling act that came with wrangling a group of energetic kids.

I barely registered the quiet footsteps behind me until a familiar presence settled beside me. Eli. Of course, it was Eli. My heart skipped, and I inwardly groaned. *Really, Carla? After all this time?*

We stood in silence, listening to the highway in the distance. I snuck a glance at him from the corner of my eye. His hands were tucked into his pockets, his posture relaxed but somehow still radiating that firefighter readiness. The fairy lights cast shadows across his face, highlighting those annoyingly perfect cheekbones.

I cleared my throat, searching for something to say that wouldn't betray the whirlwind of emotions his mere presence stirred up. But before I could speak, Eli turned slightly, his dark eyes meeting mine.

"Quite a day, huh?" he said, his voice low and warm.

I nodded, grateful for the darkness that hid the flush I could feel creeping up my neck. "Yeah, the boys were... energetic."

Eli chuckled, the sound sending an involuntary shiver down my spine. "That's one word for it. I think 'whirlwind' might be more accurate."

I couldn't help but smile, remembering the way he'd effortlessly wrangled the most rambunctious of the group. "Just five more days," I joked, then instantly wished I hadn't. Strange how I was sort of dreading the return of Rebecca and Nathan now.

We lapsed into silence again, but it wasn't uncomfortable. The cool breeze rustled the leaves. I found myself relaxing, my earlier tension melting away despite – or maybe because of – Eli's presence.

As I stood there, I couldn't help but wonder what he was thinking. Did he feel this same pull, this same confusing mix of comfort and longing? Or was I just another conquest to him, a challenge he couldn't quite let go of?

I pushed the thoughts away, focusing instead on the peaceful moment. Whatever tomorrow might bring, whatever complications our families' feud might cause, right now, in this moment, it was just us. Just Carla and Eli, standing on a porch under twinkling lights.

Eli shifted beside me, breaking the peaceful silence. "You know," he said, his voice tinged with amusement, "I think little Linc might have a future as a stunt double. Did you see that leap off the couch?"

I couldn't help but laugh, remembering the chaos from earlier. "Oh, don't remind me! I thought I was going to have a heart attack."

"Nah, you handled it like a pro." Eli chuckled, his

eyes crinkling at the corners. "Must be left over from your superhero days."

Eli's smile softened, and he turned to face me fully. The playfulness in his expression shifted to something more serious, more intense. My heart did a little twist in my chest, not dissimilar to the one Linc had taken off the sofa.

"Listen, Carla," he began, his voice lower now. He took a deep breath, and I could see the tension in his shoulders. "I think we need to talk."

I froze, my mind racing. Was this it? The moment we'd danced around for years, dodging real conversation and exchanging lingering glances? Part of me wanted to run, to hide behind the walls I'd carefully constructed. But another part, a part I'd tried so hard to silence, whispered, *Stay. Listen.*

As Eli gathered his thoughts, I found myself holding my breath, caught between hope and fear, the past and the possibility of a future I'd barely let myself imagine.

I nodded, unable to find my voice as Eli's dark eyes locked onto mine. He ran a hand through his hair, a gesture so familiar it made my heart ache.

"I owe you an apology, Carla," he said, his voice thick with emotion. "For everything that happened back then, for the way I handled it... for hurting you."

My breath caught in my throat. I'd imagined this conversation a thousand times, but nothing prepared me for the raw sincerity in his voice.

"I was a coward," Eli continued, maintaining eye contact. "I let my dad's expectations and my own insecurities dictate my actions. I should have fought for us, for you."

Tears pricked at the corners of my eyes. "Eli, I—"

He held up a hand, gently cutting me off. "Please, let me finish. I need you to know this."

I nodded, my heart racing so fast I was sure he could hear it.

"You were never just a high school crush, Carla," Eli said, his voice dropping to almost a whisper. "You were... you are... so much more than that."

Memories flooded my mind – stolen kisses under the bleachers, shared laughter over inside jokes, the devastation when it all fell apart. The sweet mingled with the painful, a bittersweet cocktail of emotions I'd tried so hard to forget.

"I've carried you with me all these years," Eli admitted, his usual cocky demeanor stripped away, leaving him vulnerable in a way I'd never seen before. "Every date, every choice... I've always measured it against what we had, what we could have had."

Oh, Eli. If he only knew how many times I'd done the same thing.

I opened my mouth to respond but found myself at a loss for words. How could I put into words the complex tangle of emotions his confession had stirred up?

Eli took a deep breath, his dark eyes boring into mine with an intensity that made my knees weak. "I know my dad's expectations have always been a cloud hanging over us, but I'm done letting that control my life. You're worth any risk, Carla. Any fight."

My breath caught in my throat. The old Eli, the one who'd always seemed content to play the role of small-town bad boy, was nowhere to be seen. In his place stood a man willing to defy everything for... me?

"I'm not asking for forever right now," he continued, his voice low and earnest. "Just a chance. A real chance, without the baggage of our families weighing us down."

A tiny spark of hope flickered to life in my chest, fragile but undeniably there. I wanted to believe him, wanted it so badly it almost hurt.

But my inner voice, ever the skeptic, piped up. *Oh sure, Carla. Because people really change, right? How many times are you going to let that charming smile sucker you in?*

I bit my lip, wrestling with the conflicting emotions. "Eli, I... I don't know what to say. This is all so sudden."

He nodded, a flicker of understanding passing across his face. "I know. I'm sorry if I'm over- whelming you. I just... I can't keep pretending anymore. This week with you just reinforced how much I've been lying to myself about my feelings."

My heart did a lazy somersault at his words. How long had I yearned for this kind of validation? To know that I wasn't alone in carrying the weight of our past?

But trust... that was the real issue, wasn't it? Could I truly open myself up again, risk my heart to the man who'd already broken it once?

I took a shaky breath. "It means more than you know to hear you say all this. But I'd be lying if I said I wasn't scared. We have so much history, so much..."

"Baggage?" he supplied with a wry smile.

I couldn't help but chuckle. "Yeah, baggage."

"Mountains of it," he agreed.

"The airport in Indy's got nothing on us."

As I trailed off, Eli reached for my hand. His touch was gentle yet firm, his calloused firefighter's fingers wrapping around mine with a warmth that contrasted sharply with the cool evening air. The simple gesture sent a jolt through me, grounding me in the present moment and creating an unexpected sense of intimacy between us.

"I know we've got a lot to work through," Eli said softly, his dark eyes fixed on mine, "but I'm willing to unpack every piece of that baggage with you, if you'll let me."

My heart raced, and I found myself torn between the urge to pull away and the desire to lean into his touch. "And what if we open those bags and find nothing but moths and regrets?" I quipped, trying to mask my vulnerability with humor, taking the metaphor too far.

Eli's lips quirked into that infuriatingly charming half-smile. "Then we'll build a better wardrobe together."

I rolled my eyes but couldn't suppress a small laugh. "Always with the smooth comebacks, aren't you, Wells?"

My mind was a whirlwind of emotions. Part of me wanted to throw caution to the wind and dive headfirst into whatever this was. But the cautious teacher in me, the one who'd learned the hard way about second chances, hesitated.

Should I trust my head or my heart? I wondered, acutely aware of the warmth of Eli's hand still enveloping mine. The fairy lights above cast a soft glow on his face, highlighting the sincerity in his eyes, and I felt my resolve weakening.

Taking a deep breath, I made my decision. I squeezed Eli's hand, a gentle pressure that spoke volumes. "Okay," I said quietly. "Let's... let's try unpacking together. But, Eli, I swear if you break my heart again, I'll sic my dad and his ancient family feud on you faster than you can say 'false alarm.'"

Eli's answering grin was equal parts relief and mischief. "Noted. Though I gotta say, facing down your dad might be scarier than any five-alarm fire I've tackled."

As we stood there, hand-in-hand on the porch, I felt a flicker of hope ignite within me. It was terrifying and exhilarating all at once, like standing on the edge of a cliff, ready to take the plunge. But with Eli's steady presence beside me, I found myself thinking that maybe the fall might be worth it.

I couldn't help but chuckle at Eli's quip about my dad. "Oh please, you fought off Mrs. Henderson's rabid chihuahua last week. I think you can handle one grumpy Putnam."

Eli's eyes sparkled with amusement. "Hey now,

Cujo Junior was a formidable opponent. I still have the battle scars to prove it." He dramatically lifted his pant leg, revealing a tiny scratch that was barely visible.

I rolled my eyes but couldn't suppress my grin. "My hero," I deadpanned.

As we stood there, the conversation naturally drifted to lighter topics. The cool evening air carried the faint scent of autumn, reminding me of crisp fall days back in high school.

"Remember that time in senior year when you convinced half the football team to help you toilet paper Coach Miller's house?" I asked, unable to keep the laughter from my voice.

Eli's eyes widened in mock innocence. "I have no idea what you're talking about, Miss Putnam. I was a model student."

"Oh really?" I arched an eyebrow. "So I suppose it was some other Elijah Wells who got caught red-handed with a roll of Charmin in one hand and a carton of eggs in the other?"

He threw his head back and laughed, the sound rich and warm. "Okay, you got me. But in my defense, Coach made us run extra laps that week because Nathan missed practice for a college visit. Talk about misplaced anger."

As we continued to reminisce, I found myself inching closer to Eli, drawn in by the familiar cadence of our banter.

"What about you, Miss Goody Two-Shoes?" Eli teased, his shoulder now brushing against mine. "Any secret rebellious streaks you want to confess?"

I felt a blush creep up my cheeks, remembering a particular incident. "Well, there was that time I may have 'borrowed' Mr. Simmons' toupee and hidden it in the biology lab skeleton..."

Eli's jaw dropped in mock horror. "Carla Putnam! I'm shocked and appalled." His voice shifted. "And also incredibly impressed."

As our laughter subsided, I realized how easy it was to fall back into our old rhythm. It was like no time had passed at all, yet so much had changed. The space between us had shrunken considerably, and I found myself hyper-aware of Eli's presence – the warmth radiating from his body, the faint scent of smoke that always seemed to cling to him.

Did he feel it too, this magnetic pull between us? I sneaked a glance at his profile. The sincerity I saw in his eyes earlier hadn't faded.

"Eli, I..." I started, my voice catching. Get it together, Carla, I chided myself. Taking a deep breath, I met his gaze. "I want to see where this could go – where we could go."

My words came out steadier than I felt, filled with a determination that surprised even me. But as I watched Eli's face light up, I knew I meant every word.

"You mean it?" he asked, a hint of that trademark cockiness creeping back into his voice. "Because I gotta warn you, I'm pretty irresistible. You might fall head over heels for me."

I rolled my eyes but couldn't help the smile tugging at my lips. "Don't push your luck. I said I'd give us a chance, not that I'd swoon at your feet."

But even as I bantered back, a part of me wondered if it was already too late. Had I ever really gotten over Eli Wells? Or had I just been running from the possibility of getting hurt again?

As those thoughts raced through my mind, Eli's arms encircled me, pulling me into a tender embrace. The warmth of his body contrasted with the cool evening air, sending a shiver down my spine. I hesitated for a split second before melting into his chest, my arms wrapping around his waist.

"You okay?" Eli murmured, his breath tickling my ear.

I nodded against his shoulder, inhaling the faint

scent of smoke and pine that seemed to cling to him. "Just... processing," I admitted.

He chuckled softly. "Yeah, me too. Never thought I'd be standing here with you like this again."

As we stood there, bathed in the soft glow of the fairy lights above us, I felt a sense of peace wash over me. It was like coming home after a long, exhausting journey. But a nagging voice in the back of my head wouldn't let me fully relax.

What if this doesn't work out? What if our families try to tear us apart again?

Eli must have sensed my tension because he pulled back slightly, his dark eyes searching mine. "Hey, what's going on in that head of yours, Putnam?"

I bit my lip, debating whether to voice my fears. "It's just... are we crazy for doing this? With our families and everything?"

He grinned, that infuriating, heart-flipping grin. "Probably. But when have I ever let a little crazy stop me?"

I couldn't help but laugh. "Fair point. I guess we're in this together then, huh?"

"Now you get it," he said, taking my hand and giving it a reassuring squeeze. "Whatever comes next, we face it hand-in-hand."

CHAPTER 14
Elijah

I heard the patter of excited feet before I saw them. Alex, Linc, and Joey burst into my parents' kitchen like a tiny whirlwind, their faces beaming with pride as they clutched colorful construction paper in their hands.

"Uncle Eli! Look what we made!" Alex exclaimed, thrusting a card covered in glitter and crayon scribbles toward me.

I couldn't help but smile as I knelt down to their level and admired their handiwork. "Wow, guys. These are amazing. What are they for?"

Joey, barely able to contain his excitement, bounced on his toes and made what I could only assume was his attempt at a monkey sound. "For Papa! To make him all better!"

My heart squeezed a little at their innocent enthusiasm. I ruffled Joey's hair, careful not to mess up the spiky style he was so proud of. "That's really thoughtful of you. I'm sure Papa will love them."

Dad was coming home today, and we were officially the welcoming party.

As I examined each card, marveling at the creativity only kids could muster, I heard familiar footsteps enter the kitchen. I glanced up to see Carla, her presence immediately shifting something in the air. Our eyes met briefly, and I felt that familiar tug of attraction I'd been trying to ignore. No longer, though. I'd held her on the porch for a glorious twenty minutes last night.

"Well, what do we have here?" Carla's warm smile lit up her face as she joined our little huddle. "Are these masterpieces I see?"

Lincoln, usually the quietest of the bunch, gave a shy smile filled with pride and a little eye roll. "You already saw them, Miss Carla!"

Carla leaned in conspiratorially, her eyes twinkling. "You know what? I think these cards are so good, they might just have magical healing powers."

I couldn't help but chuckle at that, catching Carla's eye again. "Oh yeah? And where did you get your medical degree, Dr. Putnam?"

She raised an eyebrow. "I'll have you know, Mr. Wells, I graduated top of my class from the University of Awesome Teachers."

The boys giggled, and I felt a warmth spread through my chest that had nothing to do with soup simmering on the stove. For a moment, I let myself imagine what it would be like if this was our normal —Carla and me, surrounded by laughing kids, no family feuds or complicated histories between us.

But reality had a way of crashing back in, and I pushed the thought aside. I had to focus on helping Dad recover, not daydreaming about a future that couldn't happen. Still, as I watched Carla praise the boys' artistic skills, I couldn't quite squash the tiny spark of hope that flickered in my heart.

I couldn't help myself. Maybe it was the way Carla's eyes crinkled when she smiled, or how the afternoon sunlight caught her hair just right. Whatever it was, I found myself leaning in, pressing a quick, soft kiss to her lips.

"Eli!" Carla gasped, pulling back with wide eyes.

Too late, I remembered our audience. The boys erupted into a chorus of "Oooohs" and giggles.

"Uncle Eli and Carla, sitting in a tree!" Alex sang out, his gap-toothed grin wide. This was not what I imagined for our first kiss.

"K-I-S-S-I-N-G!" the other two joined in with glee, Joey tripping over letters without a care.

My face heated, and when I glanced at Carla, her cheeks were just as flushed. "Alright, you little rascals," I said, trying to sound stern but failing miserably, "that's enough of that."

Just then, I heard the creak of floorboards in the hallway. Dad. My stomach dropped as I realized what was coming.

The kitchen door swung open, and there he was. Harold Wells, all six-foot-two of him, filling the doorframe with his presence. The laughter died instantly. He was pale and slightly winded, obviously worn out from the trip home and the walk inside.

"Papa!" Joey, bless his oblivious little heart, ran up to him. "Guess what? Uncle Eli and Miss Carla were smoochy kissing!"

My heart sank.

I watched the storm clouds gather on Dad's face, his jaw clenching tight. The temperature in the room seemed to drop ten degrees.

"Is that so?" Dad's voice was low, dangerous.

The boys, finally catching on to the tension, fell silent. Their eyes darted between me and their grandfather, confusion written all over their faces.

I swallowed hard, frantically searching for the right words. But how do you explain a decades-old family feud to three confused kids? How do you justify your heart to a father who sees only betrayal?

Carla's hand brushed my arm, and I turned to see her giving me a reassuring smile. But I could see the worry in her eyes.

"Boys," she said, her voice gentle but firm, "why don't we go finish that puzzle we were working on?"

Alex's face lit up. "Can I do the last piece?"

"We'll see," Carla replied, already herding them toward the door. As they filed out, Carla glanced back at me, her expression hard to read.

Then the door swung closed, and I was alone with Dad.

The silence stretched between us, thick and suffocating. I cleared my throat, ready to launch into some explanation, but Dad beat me to it.

"A Putnam, Elijah?" His voice was quiet, but it cut like a knife. "Of all the women in this town, you choose a Putnam?"

I felt my hackles rise. "It's not like that—"

"Not like what?" he interrupted, his eyes flashing. "Not like you're spitting on everything this family stands for? Not like you're betraying your own flesh and blood?" Dad snapped, taking a step toward me. As he did, I noticed a slight tremor in his right hand. My heart clenched.

"Hey, easy," I said, instinctively reaching out to steady him as he stumbled slightly. "Maybe we should sit down and—"

"I don't need to sit down!" he barked, but I saw the flash of pain cross his face. He pressed a hand to his chest, and I felt a surge of panic.

"Dad, please," I pleaded, guiding him gently toward a kitchen chair. "Your heart–"

"My heart's fine," he grumbled, but allowed me to help him sit. "It's you who's lost your mind."

I knelt beside him, my firefighter instincts kicking in as I assessed his breathing. "Dad, I know you're upset, but this stress isn't good for you. Can we just... can we talk about this later?"

He glared at me, but I could see the fight leaving his eyes. "There's nothing to talk about, Elijah. You know how I feel about the Putnams."

I opened my mouth, searching for the right words, but they escaped me like smoke through my fingers. My eyes darted from Dad's scowling face to the scattered get-well cards on the counter, a stark reminder of why we were all here in the first place.

My dad was fragile right now. This was entirely the wrong time for this confrontation.

"Dad, she's just here to help out. Don't read too much into it." If he looked closely at all, he'd see that I was head over heels for this woman. And it might actually kill him.

I bit back a groan. How could I make him understand? The world wasn't as black and white as he saw it. But as I looked at him, I realized something. Behind the anger in his eyes, there was hurt. Deep, decades-old hurt.

And suddenly, I was very, very tired of this never-ending conflict.

His eyes were pressed shut, his breathing evening out. As much as I wanted to fight it out and to defend Carla's presence in my life, now wasn't the time.

Movement by the door caught my eye. There stood Alex, his young face a mask of confusion and worry. His earlier excitement had vanished, replaced by something that made my heart ache – a look of understanding far beyond his years.

I swallowed hard, trying to push down the lump in my throat. "Hey, buddy," I said, forcing a smile that felt brittle on my face. "Everything's okay. Papa and I are just having a grown-up talk."

Alex's eyes darted between Dad and me, his brow furrowed. "Are you fighting because of Carla?" he asked softly. "I like her. She makes you smile, Uncle Eli."

I felt a rush of affection for my nephew, mixed with a deep sadness. This feud was affecting more than just the adults, and seeing it reflected in Alex's concerned face made that crystal clear.

"It's complicated, Alex," I said, shooting a pointed look at my dad. "But sometimes grown-ups disagree about things. It doesn't mean we don't love each other."

Harold cleared his throat, his anger seemingly deflated by Alex's presence. "That's right, son," he said gruffly. "Now, why don't you go find your brothers? I'm sure they're up to no good without you keeping an eye on them."

As Alex reluctantly left the kitchen, I turned back to my father, feeling drained but determined. "We're not done talking about this," I said quietly. "But maybe we both need some time to cool off. We'll get out of your hair and let you settle back in. I'm glad you're home."

My mother bustled in the door, a concerned look on her face. "Harold? Why on earth are you in here? Come on, let's get you to your recliner."

My dad gave me one last look, then nodded stiffly and shuffled out of the kitchen, leaving me alone with my thoughts. I leaned against the counter, my body suddenly feeling like it weighed a thousand pounds.

"Well, that went about as well as a dumpster fire," I muttered to myself, running a hand through my hair. The adrenaline from the argument was fading, leaving me feeling hollow and exhausted.

I glanced around the kitchen, my eyes landing on the colorful cards the boys had made. They were scattered across the floor, casualties of our heated exchange. As I bent to pick them up, my fingers trembling slightly, I couldn't help but think about the irony. Here I was, a firefighter who could face down raging infernos without flinching, but a confrontation with my own father left me feeling like I was falling apart at the seams.

I stood there, surrounded by the remnants of innocence and love, feeling more lost than ever.

My mind raced with conflicting thoughts. On one hand, I wanted nothing more than to make my father proud, to finally be the son he always wanted. But on the other... there was Carla. Sweet, funny, beautiful Carla, who made my heart race in a way no one else ever had.

I sighed heavily, placing the cards on the counter. "What am I supposed to do now?" I asked the empty kitchen, not expecting an answer.

CHAPTER 15

Carla

I froze outside the kitchen, my hand hovering over the bathroom doorknob as Eli's words drifted through the doorway behind me.

"...just here to help out, Dad. Don't read too much into it."

My stomach clenched. Just last night, he'd gazed into my eyes and whispered how he'd never stopped caring about me. Now he was dismissing our connection like it was nothing more than yesterday's coffee grounds.

I should've known better. The charming fire-fighter routine, those soulful looks—it was all part of Eli Wells' playbook. And here I was, falling for it hook, line, and sinker. Again.

Swallowing the lump in my throat, I plastered on

a smile and strode into the living room where Nathan's boys were sprawled on the floor, surrounded by a sea of Legos.

"Alright, munchkins," I announced, clapping my hands. "It's time for us to get going."

Predictably, a chorus of groans erupted.

"But, Miss Carla," Linc whined, brandishing a half-built spaceship, "we're not finished!"

"Yeah," piped up Joey, his chubby cheeks flushed with indignation, "we gotta save the galaxy!"

I couldn't help but chuckle. "The galaxy will still need saving at home. Come on, space cadets. Get your stuff together so your grandpa can rest."

As I herded the boys toward the door, a whirl-wind of limbs and giggles, I caught sight of Eli emerging from the kitchen. Our eyes met for a brief moment, and I quickly looked away, focusing on Joey's wildly swinging LEGO creation.

"Whoa there, buddy," I said, ducking to avoid decapitation by plastic brick. "Let's get that master-piece to a safe landing pad, okay?"

The boys' boundless energy was contagious, momentarily pushing thoughts of Eli to the back of my mind. As Linc regaled me with a detailed description of their intergalactic adventure, complete with sound effects, I found myself genuinely smiling.

"...and then the alien queen was all like, 'Pew pew pew!'" Linc exclaimed, bouncing on the couch.

"Sounds like quite the battle." I laughed, fishing LEGO pieces out from under the couch.

As I helped Joey wiggle into his coat, my traitorous mind drifted back to Eli. The way his eyes crinkled when he laughed, how his strong hands had felt on my legs on the couch.

No. I shook my head, banishing those thoughts. I'd built up walls for a reason. No matter how much my heart did an eager little dance around him, I couldn't let myself get hurt again. Last night was just a fluke. I should have listened to my instincts.

I spent the rest of the day firmly entrenched in the boys' space adventures – and avoiding too much interaction with Eli.

"Aunt Carla?" Joey's voice snapped me back to reality. "Can you tell us a story?" I'd successfully made it to bedtime without crying. I guess Operation Don't-Let-Eli-Know-He-Broke-My-Heart: The Sequel was a rousing success.

I ruffled his hair, pushing aside my inner turmoil. "Of course, sweetie. Let's get you tucked in first."

As I settled onto the edge of Linc's bed, both boys

snuggled under their covers, I heard footsteps in the hallway. My pulse quickened, knowing it was Eli, probably coming to say good night.

I took a deep breath to steady myself. I might not be able to control how I felt, but I could control how I acted. And right now, these boys needed a bedtime story, not the mess of emotions swirling inside me.

"Once upon a time," I began, my voice steady, "in a galaxy far, far away..."

Eli ducked into the room, and my heart did a little flutter despite my best efforts. I kept my focus on the boys, determined not to let his presence derail me.

"Hey, munchkins," Eli's warm voice filled the room. "Room for one more at story time?"

"Uncle Eli!" Joey squealed, his arms flailing with excitement. "We're gonna hear 'bout space heroes!"

I glanced up, catching Eli's eye for a brief moment. His smile seemed genuine, but there was tension in his shoulders that hadn't been there earlier. He perched on the edge of Joey's bed, and I couldn't help but notice how his presence seemed to fill the small room.

"Space heroes, huh?" Eli grinned, ruffling Joey's hair. "Sounds like my kind of story. You guys are gonna grow up to be real-life heroes someday, aren't you?"

Alex puffed out his chest. "I'm gonna be a fire-fighter like you and Daddy."

"That so?" Eli's eyes twinkled. "Well, you better listen to Miss Carla's story then. Firefighters need to be good listeners."

I cleared my throat, trying to ignore the warmth that spread through me at Eli's easy way with the boys. It was moments like these that made it so hard to keep my distance. I launched back into the story, weaving a tale of brave space explorers and daring rescues.

As I spoke, my hands moved of their own accord, helping Joey into his pajama top. My fingers fumbled with the buttons, my mind split between the story and the man sitting just a few feet away. I couldn't help but wonder – if things had been different, could this have been our life? Eli and me, putting our own children to bed?

I pushed the thought away, focusing on Joey's giggles as I tickled his tummy. "And then," I continued, "the brave captain had to make a choice..."

I felt Eli's eyes on me as I spun the tale, his gaze like a physical touch. Every time I glanced his way, he was there, drinking in the scene with an intensity that made my heart skip. Stop it, Carla, I scolded myself. He's not the settling-down type, remember?

"What happened next, Miss Carla?" Linc bounced on the bed, his eyes wide with excitement.

I smiled, pushing my conflicted feelings aside. "Well, the captain had to choose between saving his crew or rescuing the alien princess."

"Save the princess!" Joey shouted, nearly toppling off the bed in his enthusiasm.

Eli chuckled, steadying the boy with a gentle hand. "Easy there, space cadet. What do you think, Alex? Crew or princess?"

As the boys debated the captain's dilemma, I couldn't help but notice how Eli had inched closer, our knees almost touching as we sat on the edge of the bed. The proximity sent a jolt through me, and I struggled to keep my voice steady.

"In the end," I continued, "the captain found a way to save everyone."

"Just like a real hero," Eli murmured, his eyes meeting mine for a brief, electric moment.

I swallowed hard, reminding myself of all the reasons I needed to keep my distance. As the last giggles faded and yawns took their place, a hush fell over the room. The soft glow of the nightlight cast shadows on the walls, and I could almost feel the weight of our history settling around us.

I tucked Joey in, smoothing his hair back from his forehead. "Sweet dreams, space explorer."

"G'night, Miss Carla," he mumbled, already half-asleep. I repeated the gesture with Linc, and then walked Alex to his room across the hall, tucking him in before slipping back out into the dim light of the living room.

I turned to find Eli's eyes on me, dark and intense. I couldn't look away. It was like being pulled into orbit, helpless against the gravity of his gaze. My heart did that familiar flip, and I silently cursed its betrayal.

Eli cleared his throat softly. "You're really good with them," he said, his voice low and husky.

"Thanks," I whispered back, forcing myself to break eye contact. "It's kind of my job."

I busied myself folding the blankets from the couch, hyper-aware of Eli's presence. When I glanced up again, he had moved to stand by the kitchen, his posture stiff and tense. His hands were clenched into fists at his sides, and I could see the muscles in his jaw working.

Why does he have to look so... ugh. I pushed the thought away, focusing on tidying the living room.

But I could feel the weight of Eli's gaze, like a physical thing pressing down on me. It was all I could do not to squirm under the intensity of it.

Part of me wanted to say something, to break this charged silence. But what could I possibly say that wouldn't make things worse? So I kept my mouth shut, pretending I couldn't feel the electricity crackling in the air between us.

"Well," I said, my voice sounding unnaturally loud in the quiet room, "I should probably head to bed."

Eli nodded, his dark eyes unreadable. "Right. Yeah." He stepped aside, giving me just enough room to squeeze past him.

As I moved through the doorway, I caught a whiff of his cologne—a mix of woodsy and spicy that made my stomach do a little flip. Traitor, I scolded it silently.

"So, um," Eli started, following me into the hallway. "Rebecca and Nathan are coming back on Sunday, right?"

I nodded, grateful for the neutral topic. "Yeah, their flight gets in around noon. I promised to pick them up."

"That's... nice of you," he said, his words stilted and formal. It was like we were strangers making small talk at a bus stop, not two people with years of history between them. Two people who'd kissed earlier.

"You've got a shift at the station tomorrow, don't you?" I asked, desperate to keep the conversation going, even as I berated myself for prolonging this awkward dance.

"Yeah, bright and early," Eli confirmed, running a hand through his dark hair. "And then Thanksgiving dinner at my parents' on Thursday."

We stood there for a beat too long, the silence stretching between us like a chasm neither of us knew how to cross. I found myself wondering what he was thinking, if he was as conflicted as I was. But I squashed that thought ruthlessly. It didn't matter. It couldn't matter.

I retreated to my room, my hand trembling slightly as I closed the door behind me. The soft click of the latch felt like a gunshot in the quiet hallway, and I leaned against the wood, letting out a shaky breath.

I pushed off the door and paced the bedroom. My mind was a whirlwind, replaying every moment of the day on an endless loop. Eli's words echoed on repeat. *It's not like that.*

And yet... I wanted it to be exactly like that. I

wanted him to tell his dad to shove it. I wanted him to choose me. And he hadn't. And even with my heart bruised and bleeding from the knowledge that I cared way more about him than he did about me, I still had to physically restrain myself from tucking myself into his arms tonight.

I flopped onto the bed, staring up at the ceiling fan as it lazily spun above me. "Why does he have to be so... Eli?" I groaned, throwing an arm over my eyes.

The memory of his gentle interactions with the boys tugged at my heart. It was so at odds with the image I'd built up of him as the town playboy. I'd seen a glimpse of the man he could be—caring, attentive, patient. The kind of man I'd always dreamed of having a family with.

I sat up abruptly. I wasn't doing this again. He made his choice. I heard him talking to his dad. *It's not like that. She's just helping out.*

But even as I tried to convince myself, I couldn't shake the feeling that there was more to the story. The way he'd looked at me when we said good night... it was like he was trying to tell me something without words.

I shook my head, trying to clear it. It didn't

matter. I was leaving in a few days. Back to my life, my students, my...

I trailed off, realizing I couldn't think of anything else waiting for me back home that felt as vibrant and alive as the past few days had been. Even with all the tension and complicated history, being here—being around Eli—made me feel more like myself than I had in years.

I punched my pillow into shape with more force than necessary. I was just... nostalgic. That's all this was. Nostalgia and... really impressive biceps.

I flopped back down, willing sleep to come and silence the conflicting voices in my head. But as I drifted off, one thought kept circling: How was I supposed to keep my distance when everything in me wanted to draw closer?

CHAPTER 16

Elijah

I stepped into the dining room, a mountain of mashed potatoes in the bowl I held. The tension hit me like a wall of heat from a burning building. Dad sat at the head of the table, his stern expression unyielding. Great. This was going to be about as fun as a root canal.

Carla had offered not to come. I probably should have said yes, but she was pulling away from me and I hated it. I wasn't even sure why, but she'd been distant ever since my dad found us K-I-S-S-I-N-G. Something I hadn't gotten the pleasure of repeating. An unfortunate situation I was desperate to remedy. Shamelessly, I'd used the boys to convince her to come to Thanksgiving dinner.

"Watch out, coming through with a dangerously

buttery load of carbs," I announced, trying to inject some levity into the atmosphere. The joke fell flatter than a pancake run over by a fire truck.

As I set down the bowl, my eyes darted to Carla. She gave me a small, encouraging smile that made my heart leap. Focus, Wells. I had a minefield to navigate.

I sank into the chair next to Carla, resisting the urge to touch her. The faint scent of her perfume – something floral begging me to lean closer and investigate further – mingled with the scent of garlic and rosemary at the table. "So, uh, who's ready to dig in?" I asked, reaching for the serving spoon. "These mashed potatoes aren't going to eat themselves."

Dad cleared his throat. "Elijah, perhaps we should say grace first." His voice was chilly and slightly exasperated, an unspoken commentary on my intelligence tangled in the tone.

Right. Of course. I'd forgotten prayer in my eagerness to break the ice.

As Dad began to pray, I snuck a glance at Carla. Our eyes met, and in that brief moment, a thousand emotions passed between us. The weight of our shared history, the lingering what-ifs, the forbidden nature of... whatever this was. It was all there, simmering just beneath the surface.

I bowed my head, but my mind was far from the prayer. How had I ended up here, torn between family loyalty and the undeniable pull I felt toward Carla? And more importantly, how was I going to make it through this meal without setting off the powder keg of tension that surrounded us?

"Amen," Dad finished, his voice cutting through my thoughts.

"Amen," we all echoed.

As the dishes began to circulate, Carla's arm brushed against mine when she reached for the gravy boat. The brief contact sent a jolt through me, like touching a live wire.

"So, Carla," my mother said, cordially, "how are things at the school? I heard you guys are putting on a play soon."

Her eyes lit up, and I felt a warmth spread through my chest. Maybe this could work after all. "Oh, yes! The kids are so excited. We're doing 'The Wizard of Oz' this year."

"That's great," I replied, genuinely interested. "I bet you're an amazing director. You always did have a knack for bossing people around." Okay, I couldn't resist a little teasing.

Carla laughed, the sound like music in the otherwise silent room. "I prefer to think of it as 'gentle guidance,'" she retorted, her eyes twinkling.

I grinned, about to fire back with another quip, when I caught sight of my dad's disapproving frown. Right. The feud. The reason Carla and I weren't supposed to be within ten feet of each other, let alone exchanging playful banter at the dinner table.

The smile faded from my face as I turned my attention back to my plate, the weight of expectations settling once again on my shoulders. But as I risked one more glance at Carla, I knew that no matter how difficult things got, her presence made it all worthwhile. Now, if I could just figure out how to navigate this minefield without blowing everything up in the process.

The moment was short-lived. Dad cleared his throat, drawing everyone's attention as he picked up the carving knife. "That's enough chatter," he said gruffly. "Time to serve the turkey."

I watched as my father began carving, his movements precise and practiced. But I couldn't help noticing how his eyes kept darting toward Carla, a hint of disdain in his gaze. My stomach churned, a mix of frustration and disappointment.

"You've outdone yourself this year, Mom," I said,

trying to keep things civil. "The turkey looks perfect."

Dad grunted in response, barely acknowledging me as he continued carving. I felt torn, wanting to defend Carla but also desperate for even a scrap of approval from my father.

Dad placed a slice of turkey on Carla's plate, his lips tightening into a thin line. I held my breath, silently willing him to be polite. But he said nothing, moving on to the next plate without a word.

I caught Carla's eye again, seeing a flicker of hurt before she masked it with a polite smile. In that moment, I wanted nothing more than to reach out and take her hand, to tell her that she didn't deserve this treatment. But I knew that would only make things worse.

So instead, I turned to the kids, forcing a grin onto my face. "What are you thankful for this year, Alex?" I asked, desperate for any distraction from the growing tension.

As the children eagerly chimed in, I listened to their adorable perception of the past year, while acutely aware of the divide at our table – the innocence of the kids, the warmth of Carla, and the cold disapproval radiating from my father. And there I sat, caught in the middle, a firefighter who couldn't figure out how to douse this particular flame.

The clinking of silverware against plates filled the air, punctuated by the occasional murmur of conversation. I stabbed at my mashed potatoes.

"So, how're the boys at the fire station, Eli?" my mom asked, clearly grasping for a safe topic.

I swallowed a mouthful of turkey. "Pretty good. We've got a new trainee starting next week. Kid's eager, but green as grass."

Dad grunted. "Hope you're not coddling him. A fireman needs to be tough."

I bit back a sigh. Even my job wasn't safe territory anymore. "We'll whip him into shape, don't worry."

An awkward silence fell, broken only by Joey asking for more rolls. I caught Carla's eye across the table, and something in her expression made my heart skip a beat. She took a deep breath, and I knew what was coming.

"Mr. Wells," Carla said, her voice steady despite the slight tremor in her hands, "I wanted to thank you for having me over. It means a lot, considering... well, everything."

I held my breath, silently cheering her on. That's my girl, I thought, before catching myself. She wasn't mine, not really. But I couldn't say I didn't admire her courage.

Dad's eyes narrowed slightly. "Well," he said gruffly, "it wasn't like I was given a choice. And I suppose the boys do seem rather attached to you." He wasn't wrong. The boys had all circled around Carla since we arrived, asking her for help with their puzzles, buttering their roll, or simply pulling her through the house to show off their favorite parts about Mimi and Papa's.

I winced internally. It wasn't exactly a warm welcome, but it was something. I watched Carla's face, seeing the mix of disappointment and determination there.

"I was hoping," she pressed on, "that maybe we could talk about—"

"More turkey, anyone?" Dad interrupted, his tone brooking no argument.

I felt a surge of frustration. "Dad," I started, but he silenced me with a look.

The tension at the table ratcheted up another notch. I wanted to say something, anything, to ease it. But what could I say that wouldn't make things worse? I was a firefighter, for crying out loud. I was supposed to be good at handling hot situations. But this? This felt like trying to put out a wildfire with a squirt gun.

As Dad busied himself with the turkey, pointedly ignoring Carla's attempt at conversation, I caught her eye again. I tried to convey my admiration and support in that glance, hoping she could see how proud I was of her for trying. She gave me a small, sad smile in return, and I felt my heart twist.

I could love this woman, I realized with a jolt. The thought hit me like a bucket of ice water. And I was letting her slip away because I was too scared to stand up to my own father.

This feud had gone on long enough. It was time to put out this fire, once and for all. I just hoped I was up to the task.

I wanted nothing more than to reach out, to cover her hand with mine and offer some comfort. But I could feel my father's eyes on me, watchful and disapproving. The weight of his expectations pressed down on me like a physical thing.

Oh, forget it, I thought. I was a firefighter. I ran into burning buildings for a living. Surely, I could handle holding a girl's hand at dinner.

But as I shifted, ready to make my move, my elbow knocked into my water glass. It tipped, sending a small flood across the tablecloth.

"For Pete's sake, Elijah," my father grumbled as I scrambled for napkins.

And just like that, the moment was gone.

As I dabbed at the spreading water stain, a commotion erupted at the other end of the table. The kids were squabbling over the last dinner roll, their voices rising in pitch and volume.

"I saw it first!" Alex insisted, clutching the bread-basket protectively.

"Nu-uh!" Linc shot back, making a grab for it. "I called dibs!"

Joey, not to be outdone, piped up, "But I'm the littlest! I should get it!"

I couldn't help but chuckle, grateful for the distraction. "Alright, munchkins," I said, adopting my best authoritative voice. "How about we split it three ways? Fair's fair."

The kids considered this for a moment, then nodded in agreement. As I divvied up the bread, I caught Carla's eye. She was smiling, a real smile that reached her eyes and had my heart racing.

"Nice save," she said, her voice warm with amusement.

I grinned back, feeling some of the tension in my shoulders ease.

For a second, it was like we were the only two

people in the room. The laughter of the kids faded into the background, and I was struck by how right it felt to have Carla here, in my family's home. Despite the awkwardness, despite my father's disapproval, despite everything... she fit.

"What?" Carla asked, her eyebrows quirking up in that way they did when she was curious.

I realized I'd been staring. "Nothing," I said quickly, then added, "Just thinking about how good you are with the kids."

A flicker of vulnerability crossed her face. "They make it easy," she said softly. "They don't care about old feuds or family drama. They just... love."

In that moment, I saw past the tough exterior Carla usually presented to the world. I saw the woman who cared deeply, who wanted a family of her own someday. And I realized, with a clarity that scared me a little, that I wanted to be that family.

"Yeah," I agreed, my voice a little rough, "we could learn a thing or two from them, huh?"

Carla nodded, her eyes never leaving mine. There was understanding there, and something more.

Dad's chair scraped horribly against the floor as he shoved away from the table, jolting me from the moment. His back was all I could see as he stormed into the kitchen.

Silence descended on the room, even the kids feeling the weight of his disapproval. A surge of determination rose within me. I couldn't keep ignoring the elephant in the room – this feud that had torn our families apart for so long. Watching Carla interact with my nephews, seeing the warmth in her eyes and the easy way she fit into our chaotic family dynamic, I knew I had to do something.

"Dad," I called out, my heart racing as I stacked plates and followed him into the kitchen. "Don't be like this. Can't you just try to see Carla the way I do?" The silence that followed was deafening. I could practically hear my dad's jaw clenching from across the room. He pushed past me and back into the dining room. Stubborn as ever, I followed him, pleading my case.

"I told you to stay away from that family," he finally snapped at me.

"For crying out loud, Dad!" I exploded, frustration boiling over. "This isn't the Capulets and the Montagues! We're talking about Carla, not some faceless enemy."

Dad's laugh was bitter. "You think that makes it better? That woman's grandfather—"

"Her grandfather, Dad. Not her." I ran a hand through my hair, exasperated. "Carla's one of the kindest people I know. She volunteers at the animal shelter, tutors kids for free. She bakes cookies for your grandkids, for crying out loud!"

"Don't you dare try to use those boys to justify this... this madness," Dad growled. "You know how I feel."

I sighed. "Yeah, I do. But, Dad, Carla's not her family. She's just... Carla. And I..." I swallowed hard, realizing I was about to say something I'd never said aloud before. "I think I might love her."

His jaw clenched as he delivered the blow I'd been dreading. "You think you're in love? You don't know the first thing about commitment. You're just chasing another thrill, like always. When are you going to grow up and stop embarrassing this family?"

His words hit me like a sucker punch, stealing the air from my lungs. My face flushed with anger and shame. My fists clenched at my sides as I fought to keep my voice steady. "That's not fair, Dad. You have no idea how hard I've worked to—"

"All you've done is undermine, disrespect me, and disappoint me."

I reared back as though I'd been slapped. "Wow. Tell me how you really feel, Dad." Judging by the pain in my chest, sarcasm sucked as a shield, but it was the only one I had.

Dad's eyes widened, and for a heartbeat, I thought he might start yelling again. But then his shoulders sagged, and he let out a long, shaky breath. I watched as my father's gaze drifted to the window, his eyes glazing over with memories I couldn't see. The kitchen suddenly felt too small, too warm.

"What happened between Grandpa and Kenny Putnam, Dad?" I asked softly. "There's got to be more to this feud than just a business disagreement."

Dad's jaw clenched, and I saw a flicker of something raw and painful cross his face. "That man..." he started, then shook his head. "We were friends once, you know. Best friends. And then his..." His voice cracked, and I felt my chest tighten.

"Dad, you don't have to—"

"No, you need to understand," he insisted, meeting my eyes with an intensity that made me want to look away. "We were best friends. But sometimes things happen that can never be undone."

I leaned back on my heels, processing this new information. "But, Dad, whatever happened was decades ago. Carla had nothing to do with—"

"You sound just like your mother," he muttered.

I took a deep breath, steeling myself. "Look, I get

that you're worried. But I'm not a kid anymore. I know what I feel for Carla is real." I stood up, pacing the small kitchen. "She makes me want to be better, you know? Not just as a firefighter, but as a person."

Dad scoffed walking back through to the dining room, but I pressed on, following him. "I know you've got your reasons for hating the Putnams. But Carla's different. She's kind and smart and she challenges me in ways no one else ever has." I turned to face him, my heart pounding. "I'm not asking for your blessing, Dad. But I am asking you to try to understand."

My father stared at me for a long moment, his expression unreadable. "You're stubborn as a bull, you know that?"

I couldn't help but crack a small smile. "Gee, I wonder where I got that from…"

Dad's eyes narrowed predictably, like they did every time my mouthy comebacks slipped out.

I kept talking. No one ever said I knew when to fold 'em. "It's been years. Don't you think it's time to bury the hatchet?"

"The only place I'd like to bury a hatchet is in Jim Putnam's—"

"Harold!" my mom cut him off, shooting a pointed look at the kids.

I caught Carla's eye, seeing a mix of gratitude and anxiety there. I wanted to tell her it would be okay, that we'd figure this out together, but the words stuck in my throat.

Dad disappeared up the stairs, grumbling to himself.

I debated following him. He was so darn stubborn, he couldn't even have a conversation about this stupid feud. I should stomp up the stairs after him and corner him until he saw reason. But I wouldn't do that, because as much as I wanted to talk some sense into my dad, I also still wanted him to look at me with approval in his eyes for once, instead of disappointment.

Instead, I focused on clearing the table, my movements deliberate as I tried to sort through the mess in my head. How was I supposed to build a future with Carla if our families couldn't even be in the same room? The challenge seemed insurmountable. I glanced at her again, helping my mom pack up leftovers.

"You know," I said, sidling up to Carla at the sink, "I meant what I said. About getting our families past this stupid feud."

She raised an eyebrow, a small, sad smile playing on her lips. "Oh yeah? And how exactly do you plan on making that happen, Eli the miracle worker?"

I grinned, feeling some of the tension ease. "I have my ways." I just didn't know what those ways might possibly be in this case yet.

Carla rolled her eyes, but I caught the hint of a real smile. "Well, if anyone can do it, I suppose it would be you. Just... be careful, okay? I don't want to cause more problems for your family."

"Hey," I said softly, meeting her gaze, "you're not causing problems. You're worth fighting for."

The vulnerability in her eyes nearly took my breath away. Did she not understand how special she was? I pulled her into my arms. It was the best way I knew to show her. It wasn't enough, not nearly, but it was heaven. For a moment, we just stood there, the rest of the world fading away.

"You shouldn't give up so much for me, Eli."

"I should have fought for you when I was seventeen, Carla. I'm not making that mistake again," I promised. "It's my dad's own problem that he can't see how amazing you are."

She shook her head, obviously disagreeing with me. I held her tighter, vowing that I would tell her every day until she believed me.

Alex came barreling into the kitchen, breaking

the spell. "Uncle Eli! The football game is about to start!"

I laughed, ruffling his hair. "Okay, buddy. I'll be right in."

I was nowhere near ready to let Carla out of my arms, but Thanksgiving wasn't over yet. And I wasn't going to let Harold Wells chase Carla out of the house. Let him stew upstairs all afternoon for all I cared. My family was celebrating the holiday. And from here on out, my family included Carla.

CHAPTER 17

Carla

The old wooden boards creaked under my feet as I stepped onto the porch. Eli followed close behind, his presence both comforting and nerve-wracking. As we settled into the quiet evening, I couldn't help but feel like we were stepping into some kind of liminal space, suspended between our complicated past and an uncertain future. Thanksgiving with his parents had been... well, it wasn't the most relaxing holiday I'd ever shared.

Eli's hand brushed my arm, and I followed his pointing finger to where a deer was emerging from the trees behind the yard. My breath caught in my throat. It was such a small thing, but the fact that he wanted to share this moment with me made my heart do a little flip.

"Beautiful," I whispered, not just meaning the deer.

"Yeah," Eli murmured, his eyes still on me.

We sat down on the porch swing, the gentle sway slowing the rhythm of my racing pulse. A cool breeze carried the scent of pine, and I pulled my cardigan tighter around my shoulders, trying to ward off a shiver that had nothing to do with the temperature.

"Cold?" Eli asked, already starting to shrug off his jacket.

"I'm fine," I said quickly. The last thing I needed was to be enveloped in his scent, his warmth. It would make it even harder to keep my guard up. He laid the jacket over my lap.

As we rocked back and forth, I sneaked glances at Eli's profile. The strong line of his jaw, the slight furrow between his brows—he looked deep in thought. Part of me wanted to reach out and smooth away that worry line, but I kept my hands firmly in my lap, fingering the seams of his jacket.

My mind raced with all the things I wanted to say, all the questions I needed answered. But the weight of our families' feud, of years of complicated history, seemed to press down on my chest, making it hard to form the words.

So we sat in silence, the only sounds the creaking of the swing and the rustling of leaves in the breeze. It was oddly peaceful, despite the tension thrumming between us. In that moment, I could almost pretend we were just two people enjoying a quiet evening together, with no baggage or expectations.

But reality had a way of creeping in, even in moments like these. As another cool gust of wind swept over us, I couldn't suppress a small shiver. Eli immediately shifted closer, his warmth radiating against my side.

"You sure you're not cold?" he asked again, his voice low and gentle.

I turned to look at him, finding his face much closer than I expected. Those dark eyes of his seemed to see right through me, past all my carefully constructed defenses. And just like that, I felt myself start to crumble.

I shook my head, managing a small smile. "I'm fine. Just..." I trailed off, not sure how to finish that sentence.

I took a deep breath, my gaze drifting back to the dark silhouettes of the trees. "Eli," I began, my voice barely above a whisper. "What are we doing?"

From the corner of my eye, I saw him stiffen slightly. "What do you mean?"

I swallowed hard, forcing myself to continue. "This... us. Our families. The feud." The words tumbled out, gaining momentum. "We can't just pretend it doesn't exist. That it doesn't affect every-thing between us."

As I spoke, I felt Eli's eyes on me, intense and unwavering. His expression softened, and without a word, he reached for my hand. His touch was gentle, almost hesitant, as if he feared I might pull away. But I didn't. I couldn't. The warmth of his fingers inter-twined with mine sent a familiar spark through my body, a bittersweet reminder of what we once had – and what we could still have, if only...

His thumb traced small circles on the back of my hand. It was such a simple gesture, yet it spoke volumes. Here was the Eli no one else got to see, the one who could make me feel safe and understood with just a touch.

I took a shaky breath, feeling the weight of years of unresolved frustration pressing down on me. "It's just... do you ever wonder what might have been? If our families weren't..." I trailed off, unable to find the right words.

"At each other's throats?" Eli supplied, a hint of

his usual humor in his voice. But I could hear the underlying tension, the pain that mirrored my own.

I nodded, feeling a lump form in my throat. "Yeah. That." I paused, gathering my courage. "Sometimes, I feel like I'm being torn in two, Eli. I love my family, I do. But loving you..." The words hung in the air between us, heavy with implication.

Eli's hand tightened around mine, and I could feel him shift closer on the swing. "I know," he murmured. "Believe me, I know."

I turned to look at him then, really look at him. In the soft glow of the porch light, I could see the conflict in his dark eyes, the same struggle I felt every day reflected back at me. My heart ached with the familiarity of it all.

"Remember when your dad caught us under the bleachers?" I asked, my voice wavering slightly. "I thought the world was ending. And in a way, I guess it did."

Eli let out a low chuckle, but there was no real humor in it. "Yeah, that was... Dad went ballistic. I'd never seen him so angry."

I nodded, feeling the old pain resurface. "My dad wouldn't even look at me for days. And he still won't tell me what started all this in the first place."

As I spoke, I could feel the weight of our shared

history pressing down on us. The stolen moments, the secret smiles, the dreams we'd dared to dream – all of it overshadowed by a feud we didn't understand and couldn't control.

"Sometimes," I admitted, my voice barely above a whisper, "I wonder if it would have been easier if I'd never fallen for you in the first place."

The moment the words left my mouth, I regretted them. But Eli just squeezed my hand, his touch a silent reassurance. He understood. Of course he did. He always had.

I turned to look at Eli, half-expecting to see hurt in his eyes. Instead, I found a fierce determination that made my breath catch.

"Carla," he said, his voice low and intense, "I know this isn't easy. It's probably the hardest thing we've ever faced. But I believe in us. You're worth whatever obstacle I have to face. Even if it is my own family."

His words sent a spark of hope through me, even as my practical side tried to squash it. "How can you be so sure?" I asked, unable to keep the longing out of my voice.

Eli's lips quirked into that infuriating half-smile I'd always loved. "Because I'm stubborn as a mule, and so are you. And when we put our minds to something..."

I couldn't help but laugh. "We're an unstoppable force?"

"Exactly." He nodded, his eyes twinkling. But then his expression sobered. "Look, I'm not saying it'll be easy. But I think what we have is worth fighting for."

As I processed his words, Eli's gaze drifted to the tree line. His jaw tightened, and I knew he was gearing up to say something difficult.

"The thing is," he began, his voice hesitant, "it's not just about our families. I've got my own demons to wrestle with."

I waited, giving him space to continue. Eli rarely opened up like this, and I didn't want to spook him.

"My dad..." He sighed, running a hand through his hair. "He's always expected me to be just like Nathan. The golden boy, you know? And no matter what I do, I can never seem to measure up."

My heart ached for him. I'd always suspected this, but hearing him admit it was different. "Is that why you became a firefighter?" I asked gently.

Eli nodded. "At first, yeah. I thought maybe if I did something heroic enough, he'd finally see me. He was so proud of Nathan, I thought he'd be proud of me too. But then I realized I actually loved it. The adrenaline, the way it forces you to be present and make decisions in the moment... it's like nothing else I've ever experienced."

I could see the passion in his eyes as he talked about his work, and it made me fall for him all over again. But there was still a shadow there, a hint of the insecurity he usually hid so well.

"You're not the only one being torn in two. I'm just... floating in the in-between," he admitted. "Between what my dad wants me to be and who I really am. Between my family's expectations and..." he trailed off, his eyes meeting mine.

"And me?" I finished for him, my voice barely above a whisper.

I leaned closer, searching Eli's face for any sign of doubt or hesitation. My heart was pounding so hard I was sure he could hear it. "Do you really think we can make this work?" I asked, my voice trembling slightly. "Us, I mean. With everything stacked against us?"

The question hung in the air between us, heavy with hope and uncertainty. I held my breath, waiting for his response. Part of me was terrified he'd say no, that he'd decide it wasn't worth the risk. But another part, the part that had never stopped loving him, desperately wanted him to say yes.

Eli's dark eyes locked onto mine, and I saw a flicker of that familiar determination. "I don't want to make a life any other way, sweetheart," he said softly. "I only want you."

The conviction in his voice sent a shiver down my spine. "How can you be so sure?" I pressed, needing more reassurance.

A hint of that cocky grin I knew so well tugged at the corner of his mouth. "Because it's us," he said simply. "We've been fighting this for years, and look where we ended up. Right back here, together."

I couldn't help but smile at that. He had a point. No matter how hard we'd tried to stay apart, something always seemed to pull us back together.

The cool night air carried the scent of pine, wrapping around us like a promise. I took a deep breath, feeling lighter than I had in years. "Maybe we really can do this."

Eli's arm slipped around my shoulders, drawing me closer. "Of course we can," he replied, his voice a mix of determination and that familiar cocky charm. "Wells and Putnam, taking on the world. Or at least, taking on Minden, Indiana."

I laughed, nestling into his side.

The tension between us built, electric and undeniable. Eli's gaze dropped to my lips, and I felt my breath catch. My mind raced. What about all the reasons we shouldn't?

But as Eli leaned in, all those doubts faded away. His lips met mine in a kiss that was tender and passionate all at once. The warmth of his mouth against mine sent sparks through my entire body. I melted into him, my hands finding their way to his shoulders as his arms wrapped around my waist.

The world around us seemed to disappear. There was no porch, no feuding families, no complicated past. There was only Eli and me, finally letting ourselves have this moment we'd been denying for so long.

When we finally broke apart, I was breathless. "Wow," I whispered, a little dazed.

Eli's answering chuckle was low and warm. I felt it down to my toes. "Yeah," he agreed. "Wow."

As we pulled apart, I glanced up at the night sky. The stars twinkled above us, countless pinpricks of light piercing the darkness. It felt like they were bearing witness to this moment, this newfound resolve between Eli and me.

We fell into a comfortable silence then, savoring the peace of the moment. The gentle creaking of the porch swing mingled with the rustle of leaves in the breeze. Somewhere in the distance, a whip-poor-will called out, its haunting song a perfect backdrop to my swirling thoughts.

I couldn't help but marvel at how right this felt, despite all the reasons it shouldn't. My dad's words echoed in my mind— "Stay away from those Wells boys" –but for once, I pushed them aside. This was our choice, our moment.

As if reading my thoughts, Eli spoke up. "Penny for your thoughts, teach?"

"I think I could get used to this," I murmured.

Eli's fingers traced lazy circles on my arm. "What's that? My irresistible charm? My fire station muscles?"

I rolled my eyes, even though he couldn't see it. "Your humility, obviously."

We both chuckled, the sound melding with the night chorus of crickets and distant owl hoots. As our laughter faded, I found myself lost in thought again.

Love had always seemed like a battle to me, especially when it came to Eli. But now, wrapped in his arms, I realized it was more like... well, like a fire. Scary, unpredictable, but also exhilarating. And just like Eli rushing into a burning building, I knew I had to be brave enough to face the heat. I just wasn't sure I was that brave.

"I'm scared," I admitted.

"Of what, sweetheart?"

That we'll regret our choice to go against our families. That you'll regret choosing me. That we are setting ourselves up for a lifetime of drama. That we'll never resolve this stupid feud.

Those answers and a hundred more sat at the tip of my tongue. "That this moment won't last," I finally said.

Eli hummed softly. "It can't. No single moment can last forever, love. But if you'll let me in, we'll spend our lives in a thousand different moments like this one."

It sounded perfect. Almost too good to be true. My heart was snagged on his casual endearment. Love. He couldn't love me.

I pulled away, immediately missing his embrace. "You should go," I whispered.

"Go where? Is it too cold? We can go back inside." He closed the distance, trying to wrap his arms back around me.

"No, I mean..." I shook my head, trying to regain some of the clarity that his nearness had muddied. "Rebecca and your brother will be back in the morning. The boys are asleep. You should go home tonight. Get a good night of sleep before your shift and all that. I just... I need some time."

My gaze caught on his jaw as the muscles there tightened. "You want me to leave?" he asked. I nodded and created the distance between us again.

The hurt expression that crossed his face gutted me, but I knew it was the right thing to do.

"Because I'm a temptation if I stay tonight?" His words hinted at a joke, but his expression was worried.

A pained exhale escaped. "Something like that."

What if this was just the result of ten days spent in close proximity, battling the chaos of three tiny humans together? What if our families never got past their history? What if a future together just wasn't what God had planned?

I couldn't ask Eli to walk away from his family, nor did I want to walk away from mine.

As much as I wanted to press myself in close and cling to him, I knew I couldn't. Not right now. Maybe not ever.

"Talk to me, Carla. What's wrong?" he demanded, his voice full of gravel.

"Just give me some time, okay? This is all too fast. I need some space."

Eli's jaw tightened again. He glanced toward the yard, his eyes shuttering his emotions. "Sure. No problem, babe. You've got my number."

There it was. The mask he usually wore.

I hated it. I hated that I was the one making him feel insecure. It was the same expression he wore when his dad was making comments.

Reassurances waited at the tip of my tongue – promises that I would call and explanations of just how much I wanted to be with him. But I stayed silent. Because either way, we were both going to end up hurting. Whether it was the rejection of our families or the rejection of each other was just a matter of time.

I just had to decide which one I could live with.

CHAPTER 18

Carla

I plunged my hands into the soft mound of dough, pulling it out of the bowl, feeling the buttery texture as I pressed it together and smoothed it out. The kitchen counter was dusted with flour, evidence of my baking frenzy for the church Christmas program. As I shaped the dough into a ball, I tried to lose myself in the rhythmic motions, hoping they'd drown out the whirlwind of emotions threatening to overwhelm me.

I reached for the rolling pin and pressed it firmly across the dough. I'd made these cookies a thousand times, and my mind drifted to the events of the past few weeks. Nathan and Rebecca's leaving town and Harold Wells' subsequent heart attack had stirred up a hornet's nest of family drama that I'd been desperately trying to avoid. And then there was Eli...

I sighed, remembering our awkward farewell last night before his shift and my trip to the airport. Remembering other days with his crooked grin and playful wink as he headed out the door to the firehouse had sent my pulse into overdrive.

The way his fingers had lingered on mine as he took the coffee I'd brought him, the softness in his eyes when he thanked me – it all meant something. Which meant all these crazy doubts in my mind were probably a waste of time.

Eli had promised me everything. A lifetime of moments together.

And yet... I'd asked for time to sort out my thoughts.

I gripped the rolling pin tighter, pressing it across the dough with renewed determination, channeling my frustration into each roll. The familiar motions were soothing, grounding me in the present moment. For a few blissful seconds, I could pretend that my world wasn't tilting on its axis, that my heart wasn't torn between what I wanted and what I should want. I'd always done the expected thing. The right thing. The thing my parents would approve of.

At least the cookies would be good. Nothing like stress-baking to ensure perfectly chewy snicker-doodles.

As I worked, I wondered what Eli was doing right now. Was he out on a call, rushing into danger with that reckless bravery that both thrilled and terrified me? Or was he at the station, trading quips with Captain Parker and pretending not to care about anything beyond the next adrenaline rush?

The ache in my chest intensified, a familiar longing that I'd been fighting for years. It wasn't fair that he could affect me like this, even after all this time. I'd tried so hard to move on, to find someone who didn't come with a side of family feud and complicated history. But every time I thought I was making progress, Eli would flash that infuriating grin, and I'd be right back where I started.

I was hopeless. I shook my head at my own weakness. Absolutely hopeless.

I slid the baking sheet into the oven, the warmth washing over me as I closed the door. The kitchen was filled with the comforting aroma of cinnamon and sugar. I leaned against the counter, letting minutes pass as I stared, unseeing, through the oven window as the dough slowly began to spread and rise.

The stillness of the moment allowed my thoughts to wander, considering my next steps. Could I really continue this dance with Eli, or was it time to finally put our complicated past to rest? Just the thought of walking away from him had my heart wrenching in my chest.

I grabbed a dish towel, wiping my cinnamon-sugar-covered hands as I wrestled with the questions that had plagued me since I was a teen. If it wasn't for this stupid feud, the answer would be easy. Why couldn't Dad just tell me what happened? I tossed the towel aside with more force than necessary. It wasn't like I was asking for state secrets. Just a simple explanation for why the Wells and the Putnams couldn't play nice.

The family feud loomed over everything, an ever-present shadow that tainted even the sweetest moments. I couldn't help but wonder how different things might be if our families weren't locked in this ridiculous cold war. Would Eli and I have had a real chance in high school? Or were we doomed from the start, star-crossed lovers in a small-town soap opera?

Great, now I was quoting Shakespeare. Next thing you know, I'd be writing angsty poetry about firefighters and a rose by any other name.

But as much as I tried to laugh it off, the weight of unanswered questions pressed down on me. What could have possibly happened to drive such a deep wedge between our families? And why did it still matter so much, all these years later?

I glanced at the oven timer, ticking away the minutes until the cookies would be done. If only solving the mystery of the feud was as simple as following a recipe. Add one cup of truth, a tablespoon of forgiveness, and bake until golden brown and drama-free.

I took a deep breath, the scent of vanilla and cinnamon filling my lungs. The kitchen suddenly felt too small, too confining for the storm of emotions brewing inside me. Without really thinking about it, I found myself moving toward the quiet corner by the window, where the afternoon sun cast a warm glow on the worn wooden floor of my apartment.

It was time to call in the big guns.

I lowered myself to my knees next to the couch, clasping my hands together and bowing my head. It had been a while since I'd prayed like this—really prayed, not just the quick "please don't let me be late for work" kind of prayers. But desperate times called for desperate measures, right?

"God," I began, my voice barely above a whisper,

"I could really use some guidance here." I paused, struggling to find the right words. "This feud... it's tearing everything apart. My family, my relationship with Eli... even my sanity at this point."

I let out a shaky laugh, realizing how ridiculous it all sounded when laid out like that. But as I continued to pray, pouring out my fears and frustrations, I felt something shift inside me. A warmth that had nothing to do with the oven's heat spread through my chest.

I just wanted to know what to do.

A tear slipped down my cheek as my prayer poured from my heart. I wanted the truth to come to light. Could God help me uncover the truth? And... give me the wisdom to know what to do with it. I loved Elijah... And I didn't want to walk away from him. But I would, I admitted shakily, if I needed to. Was I supposed to honor my father and mother in this? Or should I walk away from them and start my life with Eli? What was I supposed to do? It felt like there was no right answer.

As I finished my prayer, I remained kneeling for a moment, soaking in the stillness. The constant whirl of thoughts in my head had quieted, replaced by a sense of calm determination. I had to find the truth, and suddenly, I knew exactly where to find it.

I stood up, brushing off my jeans and squaring my shoulders.

I surveyed the kitchen. Flour dusted the countertops, and a stack of dirty mixing bowls teetered precariously in the sink. My movements became more purposeful with each swipe of the sponge. I attacked the dishes with the same determination I planned to use to unravel this decades-old feud.

Grandma would likely be surprised to see me. But probably not as surprised as she'd be when I started grilling her about ancient history.

The thought of my sweet, silver-haired grandmother being interrogated like a suspect on a crime show made me snort with laughter. But as I dried my hands and hung up the dishtowel, a whisper of anxiety crept in.

What if Grandma Rose didn't want to talk about it, either? What if she shut me down like Dad always did?

I shook my head, banishing the doubts. This was my only hope of finding out what really happened. And it was the only way I would be able to move forward with Eli with a peaceful heart. Not that I wouldn't do it either way... I just loved him too much to walk away. Something I needed to tell him as soon as possible.

Memories of cozy winter evenings spent at Grandma's feet, listening to tales of Minden's past, flooded my mind. I could almost smell the cinnamon and nutmeg from her famous apple pie.

Maybe I should bring a peace offering. I eyed the freshly baked cookies cooling on the rack. Nothing loosened lips like sugar, right?

As I carefully packed a dozen cookies into a tin, my heart raced with anticipation. What secrets would Grandma Rose reveal? Would her stories finally explain why Dad tensed up every time he saw Mr. Wells at the grocery store? Or why Mrs. Wells always crossed the street to avoid talking to Mom?

But as I grabbed my car keys and headed for the door, I couldn't quite silence that nagging voice. Whatever Grandma Rose had to say, I had a feeling it was going to change everything.

CHAPTER 19

Elijah

The couch at the station groaned under my weight as I collapsed into it. A fender bender outside of church on this fine Sunday morning had escalated into a fist fight that sent one parishioner to the hospital. Sometimes, Christ's faithful weren't so faithful when tempers flared.

I shook my head, trying to wrap my mind around how a fender bender had turned into a sermon on self-control delivered through flying fists.

It wasn't the first time I'd seen someone lose their testimony over a dented bumper, but it didn't make it any easier.

A soft chuckle from across the room drew my attention.

"Rough call?" Hearing Nathan's voice made me

turn all the way around. He leaned against the counter, cradling a steaming mug of coffee in his hands. He always hung around the station too much, even when he was off-duty. It was one of the strains on his marriage with Becca. But seeing as he'd just spent two weeks on an island with her, he was probably in the clear.

"Welcome home, bro. Rough doesn't begin to cover it," I said, running a hand over my face. "Nothing like a Bible in one hand and a balled fist in the other to keep a guy humble, right?"

Nathan nodded knowingly, his eyes crinkling at the corners. "We're all a work in progress, my friend. Even on Sundays."

I sighed, leaning back into the couch. "Yeah, well, I'd like to see some progress in humanity. Some days it feels like the world is just getting worse. Aren't we supposed to be the light?"

Nathan took a slow sip of his coffee, then set it down on the coffee table as he took a seat next to me. "We are. But even lights flicker sometimes. It doesn't mean the light's out. It just means we've got some work to do."

"So, how was your week?" Nathan asked, pushing a second steaming mug toward me.

I wrapped my hands around it, grateful for the

warmth. "Ten days," I corrected with a crooked eyebrow. "It was good. Boys were great."

Nathan's eyebrow quirked up in return. He wasn't buying it. "Right. And that's why you look like you've been chewing on lemons all morning?"

I forced a chuckle, but it sounded hollow even to my ears. "What, a guy can't have a sour face without his big brother playing twenty questions?"

"Not when that guy is you, Eli," Nathan replied, leaning forward. His captain's voice was creeping in, the one that always made me feel like I was about to get a lecture. "Come on, spill. What's got you so wound up?"

I took a sip of coffee, buying time. How could I explain the tornado of emotions swirling inside me? The way the fight with Dad had reopened wounds I thought had long since healed? The constant tug-of-war between what I wanted and what Dad expected? The niggling fear I had that Carla was going to be the one to walk away from us this time?

"It's nothing," I muttered, but even I didn't believe it. "Just... Dad's been extra Harold-like since his heart attack. All this talk about legacy and family honor."

Nathan's face softened. "Eli, you know Dad's proud of you. You're an excellent firefighter."

I snorted. "Yeah, sure. That's why he keeps comparing me to you, the golden boy who can do no wrong."

As soon as the words left my mouth, I regretted them. Nathan's face fell, and I felt like the world's biggest jerk. Here he was, trying to help, and I was lashing out like a petulant kid.

"Sorry," I mumbled, running a hand through my hair. "I didn't mean that. It's just... complicated."

Nathan nodded, understanding in his eyes. "It always is with family. Want to talk about it?"

I hesitated, the words stuck in my throat. How could I explain something I barely understood myself?

I glanced around the station, making sure no one was within earshot. The last thing I needed was for this to become small-town gossip. Leaning in, I lowered my voice.

"It's Carla," I confessed, the name alone sending a jolt through my chest. "I can't... I can't shake her, Nate. Every time I see her, it's like I'm seventeen again, sneaking kisses under the bleachers."

Nathan's eyebrows shot up, but he didn't interrupt. I plowed on, the words tumbling out now that the dam had broken.

"I know about the feud, about Dad's issues with

her family. But there's this... connection. It's always been there, and I won't ignore it anymore. I love her," I admitted.

My brother nodded slowly, a thoughtful look crossing his face. "I get it, Eli. I always suspected it would come to this, actually."

He took a sip of his coffee, and I could see him choosing his words carefully. "Remember when Becca and I hit that rough patch?"

I snorted. "You mean this summer? Yeah, vaguely."

Nathan chuckled, but his eyes were serious. "That time apart... it nearly broke me. But fighting for her and for us? Best decision I ever made."

He leaned forward, his voice low but intense. "Love isn't always easy, little brother. Sometimes, you have to fight for it. But let me tell you, it's worth every battle."

I felt a spark of hope ignite in my chest, but doubt quickly smothered it. "It's different with Carla," I argued. "There's all this history, and all this bad blood between our families. We aren't married. Not like you and Becca."

"And you think Becca and I didn't have obsta-cles?" Nathan countered. "The point is, Eli, you can't let fear or other people's expectations hold you back from something that could be amazing."

Nathan's serious expression suddenly gave way to a mischievous grin. "Besides," he said, leaning back in his chair, "maybe Carla's exactly what you need to tame that bad boy reputation of yours."

I rolled my eyes but couldn't help the chuckle that escaped me. "Oh, come on. I'm not that bad."

"Really?" Nathan quirked an eyebrow. "Who was it that crashed Dad's car into the church sign last year?"

"That was an accident!" I protested, feeling my face heat up. "And I fixed it, didn't I?"

"After Pastor Justin caught you trying to rearrange the letters to spell out 'Holy Shift,'" Nathan countered, his eyes twinkling with amusement.

I couldn't help but laugh, grateful for the momentary reprieve from my worries. It felt good to joke around with my brother like this, even if it was at my expense.

But as quickly as it had come, the lightness faded. I sighed, running a hand through my hair. "Dad's still recovering from his heart attack. What if pursuing something with Carla sends him right back to the hospital?"

Nathan's expression softened. "Eli, you can't live your life based on Dad's expectations or his health. That's not fair to you, and it's not fair to him either."

I stared down at my coffee, watching the steam curl up from the mug. "I know, but... I just can't shake this feeling that I'll be letting him down. Again."

"Hey," Nathan said firmly, causing me to look up. "You're not a disappointment, Eli. You're a good man. Dad sees that, even if he doesn't always show it."

I wanted to believe him, but years of trying to measure up to Nathan's golden boy status made it hard. Still, his words sparked a tiny flame of hope in my chest. I thought I had smothered that little spark years ago.

I leaned back, letting Nathan's words sink in. The station chatter faded into the background as I considered everything my brother had said. It hit me then, like a blast of water from a fire hose, just how much Nathan's support meant to me.

"You know," I said, my voice a little rough, "I never thought I'd say this, but I'm glad you're here, Nate. Even if you are an insufferable know-it-all sometimes."

Nathan grinned, lifting his mug in a mock toast. "That's what big brothers are for, right?"

"Look," Nathan said, setting down his mug with a soft thud. "If you want my advice – and I know you do, even if you won't admit it – be honest with Carla. Tell her how you feel."

I snorted. "I did. She said she needs time to figure it out."

"Then trust your connection. It's clear there's still something there, even after all these years."

"Alright," I said, straightening up. "But if this blows up in my face, I'm totally blaming you. I just wish Dad would get over this stupid feud already. It's been what, forty years? You'd think he'd have let it go by now."

Nathan's expression shifted, a flicker of something – was that guilt? – passing over his face. He glanced around the station, as if checking to make sure no one was listening in.

"About that," he said, lowering his voice. "There's something you should know, Eli. Remember that Christmas when Aunt Carol came to visit from Seattle?"

I frowned, trying to recall. "Vaguely. I was working the holiday shift that year, right? Rookie duties and all that."

"Exactly," Nathan nodded. "Well, there was... an incident. A pretty big blow-up, actually."

My eyebrows shot up. "What? How come I never heard about this?"

Nathan sighed, absently tracing the rim of his coffee mug. "Dad would kill me. But I think it's time you knew the whole story."

I leaned forward, curiosity burning through me. Whatever this was, it had to be big for Nathan to look so serious. "I'm all ears, bro. Spill it."

As Nathan opened his mouth to continue, I couldn't help but wonder how this revelation might change everything – not just with Dad, but with Carla too. My heart raced, equal parts excitement and dread coursing through my veins. Whatever Nathan was about to say, I had a feeling nothing would be the same after this.

I leaned in, my elbows on the table, every muscle in my body tense with anticipation. Nathan's eyes met mine, and I saw a flicker of hesitation. But then he took a deep breath, and I knew he was about to drop a bombshell.

"Aunt Carol confronted Dad that night about the grudge he was holding against the Putnams."

CHAPTER 20

Carla

I stepped out of my car, clutching the small bouquet I'd brought for Grandma, the cellophane crinkling in my sweaty grip.

I could do this. Okay, maybe I was trying to psych myself up. It was just Grandma. Sweet, loving Grandma who definitely wouldn't spill any earth-shattering family secrets today.

My heart hammered as I made my way to the entrance of the nursing home. The automatic doors whooshed open, cool air rushing out to greet me. I breathed in deeply, the familiar scent of antiseptic tinged with a hint of potpourri filling my nostrils.

As I walked down the corridor, my sneakers squeaking on the polished linoleum, I couldn't help but notice the life buzzing around me. Elderly residents shuffled past, some with walkers, others being pushed in wheelchairs by attentive nurses. The soft hum of conversation drifted from open doorways, punctuated by occasional bursts of laughter.

"Good afternoon, Carla!" chirped a passing nurse. "Here to see Rose?"

I nodded, managing a smile. "You bet. How's she doing today?"

"Oh, chipper as always. She's been working on some new knitting project all morning."

My smile grew more genuine. That was Grandma Rose, alright. Always keeping her hands busy.

As I neared her room, my steps slowed. The questions I'd been wrestling with for weeks bubbled up again, making my palms sweat. Why had Dad been so tight-lipped about our family's history with the Wells? What could have possibly happened to drive such a deep wedge between the once-close friends?

Taking one last deep breath, I squared my shoulders and knocked on Grandma's door, ready to face whatever truths awaited me inside.

I pushed open the door and the sight of Grandma instantly warmed my heart. There she sat in her favorite armchair by the window, bathed in soft afternoon light, her nimble fingers working away at a vibrant scarf.

"Carla, sweetheart!" she exclaimed, her face lighting up. She set her knitting aside and opened her arms wide. "Come give your grandmother a hug!"

I rushed over, careful not to crush the flowers as I embraced her. The familiar scent of lavender and yarn enveloped me, and I felt like a little girl again, safe in her arms.

"Hi, Grandma," I said, pulling back with a smile. "I brought you these." I handed her the bouquet, a cheerful mix of daisies and carnations.

"Oh, they're lovely!" Grandma exclaimed, her eyes twinkling. "They'll brighten up this old room nicely."

As she fussed with the flowers, I settled into the chair across from her, my heart racing. How did someone casually bring up decades-old family drama?

"So, how've you been, dear?" she asked, turning her attention back to me.

I laughed, grateful for the easy opening. "Oh, you know, just trying to survive the daily chaos. I helped take care of my friend Rebecca's kids last week so she and her husband could take a long-overdue honeymoon. How about you, Grandma?" I asked, gesturing to her knitting. "Starting a new project?"

"Oh, this old thing?" She held up the scarf, a riot of blues and purples. "Just keeping my hands busy. You know me, can't sit still for long."

I nodded, a lump forming in my throat. It was now or never. "Grandma," I began, my voice wavering slightly, "I actually came here today because... well, because I wanted to ask you about something."

Grandma's hands stilled, her eyes meeting mine with a mixture of curiosity and concern. "What is it, dear?"

I took a deep breath, fortifying myself. "I want to know about our family's history with the Wells. Why there's been this... feud for so long."

As the words left my mouth, I couldn't help but think of Eli again. His infuriating grin, the way he always seemed to show up just when I least expected it.

I focused back on Grandma, watching as a shadow crossed her face. My heart sank. Would she even entertain the conversation? Her knitting needles lay motionless in her lap, the cheerful scarf forgotten. I watched as her expression shifted, a mix of pain and hesitation clouding her usually warm features.

"Oh, Carla," she sighed, her voice heavy. "That's quite a loaded question you're asking."

I leaned forward, my heart hammering. "I know it might be difficult, Grandma, but I need to understand. It's... it's affecting my life more than I'd like to admit."

And by 'affecting,' I meant making me question every interaction I had with a certain frustratingly handsome firefighter. But I kept that particular thought to myself.

Her eyes darted to the window, then back to me. "It's not a pleasant story, dear. Are you sure you want to hear it?"

"Please," I urged, reaching out to clasp her hand. "I can't keep living with this divide, not knowing why it exists. How am I supposed to move forward when the past keeps holding me back?"

Like keeping me from fully embracing the heart-flipping, butterfly-inducing feelings I got around Eli.

My grandmother's fingers tightened around mine, her resolve visibly wavering. "I suppose you're old enough now," she murmured, more to herself than to me. "And perhaps... perhaps it's time the truth came to light."

I held my breath, sensing we were on the cusp of something momentous. Whatever Grandma was about to reveal, I knew it would change everything.

"It all started with your grandfather," she began, her voice barely above a whisper. "Kenneth."

I remembered Grandpa Kenny a little, but he'd died when I was young.

"Kenneth was a well-respected veterinarian. And his business partner was Harold Wells, Senior."

I nodded. I had known about the business partnership falling apart, so I was following.

"Harold's daughter, Carol, worked at the clinic after school. Bookkeeping, cleaning, helping however they needed." My heart sank at the sad tone of my grandmother's voice.

"I made excuses for years, denied it to everyone and myself. But... I knew. My Kenneth slept with that girl, Carol."

I gasped, struggling to comprehend. Grandma stared out the window. "It was a scandal. Carol was young, barely out of high school, and Kenny was married with a child."

Married to Grandma, I reminded myself. My heart cracked for how hard this must be for her to recount.

"The affair itself was bad enough," Grandma

continued, her eyes growing misty. "But then Carol found out she was pregnant."

"Oh no," I whispered, my heart sinking for the younger version of my grandma who'd been betrayed by her husband.

Grandma's voice cracked as she spoke. "Kenny denied everything. He refused to acknowledge the child, left Carol to face the consequences alone. The town all but shunned her. She claimed he had pressured her, and the entire thing grew worse and worse."

I watched as a tear slipped down my grandmother's cheek, and I felt my own eyes welling up in response. The weight of decades-old pain hung heavy in the air between us.

"I can't even imagine how Carol must have felt," I said, my mind reeling. All those years of family tension, the cold silences and pointed glares... it all stemmed from this betrayal.

Grandma dabbed at her eyes with a tissue. "It tore our family apart, Carla. The pain, the lies... it was like a poison that spread through both the Putnams and the Wells."

I sat there, stunned, as the pieces of our family's broken history began to fall into place. Suddenly, all those years of tension made a twisted kind of sense.

And all I could think was: How on earth was I supposed to face Eli now?

I felt like I'd been punched in the gut. My mind raced, trying to process the bombshell Grandma Putnam had just dropped. Anger bubbled up inside me – anger at Grandpa Kenny for his cowardice, at the unfairness of it all. But mostly, I felt an over-whelming sadness for Carol and the child who never knew their father.

"What happened next?" I asked, my voice barely above a whisper.

Grandma's eyes clouded with memory. "The Wells family stood by Carol through it all. Supported her, defended her against the rumors and gossip. But your dad..."

I leaned forward, my heart hammering. "What about my dad?"

"Jim couldn't accept it," she said, shaking her head. "He refused to believe his father could do such a thing. Kenny never admitted anything. Jim called Carol a liar, said she was trying to ruin the Putnam name."

"Oh, no," I muttered, feeling sick. My own father, taking the side of a man who'd abandoned his own child. I thought of all the times Dad had spoken proudly of the Putnam family values. How could he have been so blind?

Grandma continued, her voice heavy with regret. "The friendship between Harold and Jim crumbled. The business partnership between Harold Senior and Kenny obviously fell apart. And the rest, well..." She gestured vaguely, encompassing decades of hurt and misunderstanding.

I sat back, feeling drained. All those years of feuding, of cold shoulders and muttered insults – all because of one man's betrayal and another's refusal to see the truth. And here I was, caught in the middle, my heart tugging me toward Elijah Wells despite it all.

"Grandma," I said, my voice thick with emotion, "does Dad know now? That Grandpa lied?"

I watched Grandma's face, searching for any hint of what she might be thinking. Her eyes, wise and warm, met mine with a mixture of hope and caution.

"I don't know, sweetheart," she said softly. "He loved his father... I didn't want to change that. Kenny was a decent man who made some big mistakes. But he loved Jim. How could I tarnish the man Jimmy looked up to his entire life?"

I shook my head, my mind racing. My dad was

hanging on to a lie about his dad and it was ripping my life apart.

And how could I even broach this subject with Eli? 'Hey, by the way, did you know our families have been feuding over my grandfather's affair with your aunt and the child he abandoned?' Yeah, that'd go over well. Of course Harold Wells hated my family.

If what Carol had said was true, that she'd been pressured – I pushed back the thought. One version of the truth was bad enough, but if my grandfather had been a manipulative monster in addition to being an unfaithful husband?

I'd deal with that later.

"Carla," Grandma said, reaching out to pat my hand, "I know this is a lot to take in. But maybe knowing the truth can help heal old wounds."

I let out a bitter laugh. "Heal? Grandma, this is like finding out our whole lives have been built on quicksand. How do we even begin to fix this?"

It was time to face the truth – not just about our families, but about my own feelings as well. How could I ask Elijah and his family to forgive something like a rejected child and an illicit affair?

"I have faith in you, Carla. You've always had a way of bringing people together, even as a little girl."

Her words struck a chord, and I felt a tiny spark of hope ignite in my chest. Could I really be the one to bridge this divide?

As if reading my thoughts, Grandma squeezed my hand. "It's time to put this feud behind us."

I nodded, though I wasn't sure I agreed with her. I stood up, my legs feeling like jelly beneath me. "Thanks, Grandma," I said, wrapping my arms around her frail shoulders. "For everything."

She hugged me back fiercely, her strength surprising me. "You're welcome, sweetie. Now go on, make us proud."

"I'll try," I said, planting a kiss on her cheek.

I made my way out of the nursing home, my mind a whirlwind of thoughts. The antiseptic smell faded, replaced by the crisp winter air as I stepped outside. My feet carried me toward my car, but my brain was miles away.

CHAPTER 21

Elijah

I stood in the corner of Nathan and Rebecca's living room, nursing a mug of eggnog and watching the holiday chaos unfold. The scent of fresh pine filled the air as the family bustled around the Christmas tree, hanging ornaments and tinsel with cheerful abandon. Laughter echoed off the walls, accompanied by the quiet Christmas music Rebecca had turned on the TV.

"Eli, catch!" Nathan called out, tossing a sparkly star my way. I fumbled it, nearly spilling my drink in the process. I sighed in relief that it didn't shatter on the floor.

"Nice hands," he teased.

I forced a chuckle and pretended to chuck it at his head after I picked it up, but inside I felt a pang.

Nathan was here, surrounded by his perfect family. A wife who loved him and boys who thought he hung the moon. And where did that leave me?

Still the screw-up, apparently. Couldn't even close the deal with Carla. I'd thought of nothing else since the night we'd talked on the patio. She hadn't answered my calls, and her text messages had been short and lacked all the warmth I had grown used to. I kept telling myself that she was busy with work. Meanwhile, I was on my forty-eight hours off duty. Forty-eight hours that had slowed to a complete crawl without glimpses of her during my days.

It may have only been two days since Nathan and Rebecca got home and Carla and I had moved out of this house, but a couple more days of this and I'd lose my mind.

I wanted to talk to her about what Nathan had told me. The whole thing was crazy, but I under-stood a little more about why my dad felt so strongly about her family. Still, it had been decades and Carla wasn't at fault.

Kenneth Putnam had died years ago, but the feud lived on. What a legacy.

Rebecca expertly wrangled their kids into helping with the lower branches, subtly rearranging the ornaments after they placed them. I couldn't help but notice how in sync she and Nathan seemed. The rocky patch in their marriage was clearly behind them. They moved around each other with easy familiarity, stealing quick kisses anytime they were close.

My mind drifted back to Carla and the moments we'd shared over the week together. Late night conversations on the couch, walks through the neighborhood. Her laugh as I quoted *21 Jump Street* when she talked about her classes. The way her hand would linger on my arm, eyes sparkling...

"Earth to Eli!" Rebecca's voice snapped me back to reality. "You gonna help decorate or just stand there looking pretty?"

I plastered on my trademark smirk. "Oh, my bad. I thought you invited me so I would *be* the decoration. I mean, it's a tough job looking this good, but I'm willing to make the sacrifice."

Nathan and Alex groaned in reply to my jokes, and I sighed in relief. This was familiar, at least.

As I reluctantly joined the decorating fray, I couldn't shake the feeling of being an outsider in my own family. Nathan and Rebecca's picture-perfect reunion only highlighted my own shortcomings.

I sighed, reaching for another ornament. My gaze drifted to the kitchen table, where my nephews were now hunched over gingerbread house kits, their little tongues poking out in concentration.

"Uncle Eli!" Linc called out. "Can you help me stick this roof on? It keeps falling off!"

I plastered on a smile and sauntered over. "Sure thing, buddy. Let's see what we can do about this architectural disaster."

As I helped Linc, Joey, and Alex with their wobbly gingerbread creations, my mind wandered. Would Carla and I ever have moments like this with our own kids? The thought sent a shiver of both longing and fear through me.

"You're good with them," Rebecca commented, appearing at my elbow with a mug of hot cocoa.

I shrugged, aiming for nonchalance. "Nah, I just haven't grown up myself. Makes it easy to relate."

Rebecca's knowing look told me she wasn't buying it. "I'm serious. You did great with them while we were gone. And you'd make a great dad someday. When you're ready."

Her words, meant to be encouraging, only twisted the knife of self-doubt deeper. I thought of my father's disapproving frown, his harsh words still ringing in my ears: "When are you gonna grow up and take some responsibility, Elijah? You can't coast by on your charm forever."

I swallowed hard, focusing on squeezing icing out of the bag. "Yeah, well, let's not get ahead of ourselves. I've got to master gingerbread engineering first."

Thirty sticky fingers and a deluge of sprinkles later, I stepped away from the table, handing the reins off to Rebecca. The festive chaos was becoming overwhelming. I needed air. "I'm gonna step out for a bit," I mumbled, making my way through the living room.

As I pushed open the front door, the blast of cold air hit me like a wake-up call. I inhaled deeply, letting the crisp winter night fill my lungs. The porch creaked under my feet as I moved to the railing, bypassing the swing where I'd sat with Carla. My hands gripped the weathered wood.

Out here, away from the warmth and laughter inside, I could finally breathe. But with that breath came the flood of thoughts I'd been trying to keep at bay all evening.

I closed my eyes, picturing Carla's smile, the way her eyes lit up when she laughed. God, I wanted that – wanted her – more than I'd ever admit out loud. But the image morphed, Carla's bright expression fading to disappointment. In my mind's eye, I saw myself fumbling, failing, letting her down just like I'd let down everyone else.

I couldn't even get my act together in my own fantasies.

The worst part was, I could see it all so clearly – the life we could have. Sunday dinners with both our families, Carla corralling our kids while I manned the grill. Quiet nights by the fire, her head on my shoulder as we talked about our day. But then my father's voice would creep in, reminding me of all the ways I'd never measure up.

I sighed, my breath forming a misty cloud in the cold air. I needed to face it. I was better off putting out house fires than trying to build a home.

I gripped the porch railing, feeling the bite of cold wood against my palms. The yard stretched out before me until it disappeared in the stretch of trees I'd watched with Carla on Saturday night. It was beautiful, peaceful – everything I wasn't feeling inside.

Everything inside me longed to talk to Carla, but maybe she wasn't feeling the same, judging by the unanswered calls. I should just move on.

Except, I was too stubborn for that. I wouldn't give up without a fight. Carla had asked for time, and I'd given it to her. Two days wasn't much, but time was up. And besides, with the new info about the rift between our families, maybe the situation wasn't so hopeless as before.

I just had to convince Carla to give us a shot. The feelings we shared weren't just some relic of the week we spent sharing a house. I'd never felt anything more real. And I couldn't walk away.

Two days and one long shift at the station later, I was at the Minden Christmas Market, held at the county fairgrounds. I knelt down next to a little girl with pigtails, her eyes wide as saucers as she reached for one of our plastic fire helmets.

"There you go, sweetheart," I said, gently placing it on her head. "Now you're officially part of the Minden Rogers Fire Department Junior Squad."

Her face lit up like a Christmas tree. "Really? Can I put out fires now?"

I chuckled, my heart warming at her enthusiasm. "Well, not quite yet. But you know what's even more important than putting out fires? Preventing them in the first place."

She tilted her head, curiosity sparkling in her eyes. "How do we do that?"

"Great question," I said, tapping my chin thoughtfully. "Say, do you believe in Santa Claus?"

She nodded vigorously, her pigtails bouncing.

"Well, here's a secret," I leaned in, lowering my voice conspiratorially. "Santa's pretty good at squeezing down chimneys, but he's not a fan of actual fire in the fireplace. So on Christmas Eve, make sure to tell your parents to leave the fire out. Blow out candles before bed and don't play with the stove, okay?

"Deal!" she exclaimed, beaming up at me.

As she scampered off to show her parents her new hat, I couldn't help but smile. It was moments like these that remind me why I became a firefighter in the first place. Sure, initially it was to prove something to my dad, but now? Now it's about these kids, this community. And a little about the adrenaline.

The sound of carolers warming up caught my attention, and I straightened, brushing off my knees. The familiar strains of "Silent Night" drifted across the pavilion, and I found myself humming along, scanning the festive crowd.

That's when I saw her.

Standing there in a red sweater, Carla's hair caught the twinkling lights strung up around the square. She hadn't noticed me yet, her attention on the carolers, a soft smile playing on her lips. Man, that smile. I wanted to see it every day.

I should look away. I should focus on handing

out more helmets, on being the responsible fire-fighter, on anything but her. But I couldn't. It was as if she had her own gravitational pull, and I was help-less to resist.

"Hey, Eli!" Kyle called out. "We're running low on stickers. Can you grab some from the truck?"

"Uh, yeah," I replied, reluctantly tearing my gaze away from Carla. "I'm on it."

As I turned back, my eyes instinctively sought her out again. And this time, Carla was looking right at me. The world around us seemed to blur, the festive chaos fading into a muffled hum. Her dark eyes locked onto mine, and I swore I could feel the electricity crackling between us, even from across the building.

For a moment, I forgot how to breathe. The twinkling lights, the carolers' voices, the laughter of children – it all melted away. There was only Carla, her gaze holding mine with an intensity that made my heart race.

I didn't even realize I was moving until I heard Kyle's confused voice behind me. "Eli? Where are you going? What about the stickers?"

"I, uh..." I fumbled for words, my eyes still fixed on Carla. "Cover for me for a sec, will you?"

Without waiting for a response, I stepped away

from the booth. My feet carried me forward of their own accord, weaving through the crowd. My heart pounded in my chest, a mix of anticipation and nervousness making my palms sweat.

What was I doing? I continued to push through the throng of festival-goers. This was crazy. Dad would flip if he found out. And seeing as the entire tri-county area had turned out for the Christmas Market, he would definitely hear about it.

But for once, I didn't care what my dad would think. All I knew was that I had to talk to her, to bridge this gap between us.

As I got closer, doubt started to creep in. What if she didn't want to talk to me? What if I was misreading everything? But then Carla's lips curved into a small, hesitant smile, and suddenly, none of those fears mattered anymore.

I was done letting our families' feud dictate my life. It was time to take a risk, whatever the consequences may be.

The festival's twinkling lights danced in Carla's eyes as I approached, casting a warm glow on her face. "Carla," I said, my voice coming out huskier than I'd intended.

"We need to talk about the–"

"I found out something you should know."

"Oh, you–"

"No, go ahead."

Our words tripped over one another, and we both smiled.

I stepped closer. "I missed you," I admitted softly, setting aside the rest of what needed to be said for now. My feelings wouldn't be pushed down any longer.

"Me too," she admitted, ducking her gaze away from mine.

The words tumbled out, fueled by years of pent-up emotions. "I'm terrified of disappointing my dad."

Carla's eyes widened, a hint of fear in them, but I pressed on.

"But you know what scares me even more? The thought of losing you. Again." I swallowed hard, my heart hammering against my ribs. A small voice in the back of my mind screamed, *What are you doing? You're ruining everything!* But for once, I ignored it. I was tired of being the family screw-up, tired of letting fear dictate my choices.

"I know our families have this whole Romeo and Juliet thing going on," I continued, attempting a weak smile, "but I don't care anymore. I'd give up everything if it meant I could be with you."

I held my breath, waiting for her response. The

carolers finished their song, and the only sound was the applause of the crowd and my own thundering heartbeat.

I watched as Carla's expression softened. She took a deep breath, and I braced myself for rejection.

"Eli," she began, her voice low and steady, "I've spent so long trying to convince myself that you were just the town playboy, and that what we had was nothing more than a teenage crush."

My heart sank, but then she reached out and touched my arm. The warmth of her fingers sent a jolt through me, and suddenly I was seventeen again, stealing kisses under the bleachers.

"But…" She shook her head, a wry smile playing on her lips. "I can't keep pretending."

I let out a breath I didn't know I'd been holding. "So, you're saying…"

"I'm saying that I've been comparing every guy to you for years," she admitted, rolling her eyes at herself. "And they all come up short."

A grin spread across my face, but Carla wasn't finished. Her expression grew serious, and she glanced around before leaning in closer.

"There's something you need to know about our families," she said, her voice barely above a whisper. "My family, I mean."

"I already know, sweetheart."

Carla sighed, her shoulders slumping slightly. "Then you know why your dad hates my family. You know that we deserve it."

Her words hit me like a bucket of ice water. "Carla, no. You haven't done anything wrong."

Her eyes grew glossy, and my heart cracked at the pain I saw in them. "That's why you've been dodging my calls," I murmured, the pieces falling into place.

Carla nodded. "How can I ask you to walk away from your family when mine are the ones who wronged your aunt?"

My voice was firm. "You're not asking, I'm offering. I think it's time this feud was put to bed once and for all. But if my dad can't help but hold the sins of your grandfather against you, then I don't want any part of being his family."

"You can't mean that," she argued.

"I mean every word, sweetheart. You're my family. I love you more than anything or anyone else in this world." And I would spend every single day proving that to her.

Her sweet smile reassured me that I'd said the right thing.

"I...I love you, too," she said through a laugh, her eyes wide with joy.

A rush of emotions surged through me—relief, elation, and a fierce protectiveness that made my chest ache.

I pulled her into my arms and pressed a kiss to her forehead, relishing how perfectly right she felt against me. Then, I dropped my lips to hers. Her breath hitched, soft and warm against my skin, as her fingers curled into the front of my shirt like I was her anchor in a storm. I would be that anchor, I promised myself. Nothing had ever made me confident the way her trust did.

The taste of her was a blend of sweetness and spice, sending a surge of heat straight to my chest. The buzz of the town melted into the background, replaced by the thunderous rhythm of my heart, calling to hers with every beat. I was claiming her once and for all, in front of the entire town of Minden.

And I had never been happier.

CHAPTER 22

Carla

I t was entirely possible that the night would be a disaster. What on earth had convinced me that this was a good idea in the first place?

I stood next to Eli by the Christmas tree, our hands intertwined, my palm embarrassingly sweaty against his. My heart was doing its usual gymnastics routine at his touch, but this time with an extra dose of nervous energy. We were about to face our families together, and I couldn't decide if I was more excited or terrified.

"You okay?" Eli whispered, giving my hand a gentle squeeze. His dark eyes, usually dancing with mischief, were soft with concern.

I managed a weak smile. "Just peachy. Nothing

says 'Merry Christmas' like dropping a bombshell on our feuding families, right?"

He chuckled, the sound sending a familiar warmth through me. "We've got this, Carla. Besides, if things go south, I can always escape through a window. I'll catch you if you jump after me."

I rolled my eyes but couldn't suppress a grin. "My hero."

The living room of Nathan and Rebecca's home was a Christmas paradise. Twinkling lights adorned every surface, casting a soft glow over the festive decorations. The tree beside us was a masterpiece of ornaments and tinsel, and the aroma of fresh-baked cookies and cinnamon hung in the air. It was picture-perfect, and I found myself wishing we could freeze this moment before the potential chaos ensued.

Rebecca bustled in from the kitchen, flour dusting her cheek. "Everything okay, you two?" she asked, her eyes flickering between us knowingly. "You look like you're about to face a firing squad," she teased, coming over to adjust a drooping ornament.

Eli snorted. "Just the two most stubborn men in Minden about to find out their kids are dating. No big deal."

I elbowed him gently. "Your optimism is over-whelming, Eli."

"We'll be fine, Becca," Eli replied, his trademark grin sliding into place. "I was just admiring your Martha Stewart-worthy decorations."

Nathan appeared behind her, Joey perched on his hip, cookie in hand. "Don't let her fool you," he stage-whispered. "Half of this was from the dollar store."

"Nathan!" Rebecca swatted at him playfully, but her eyes were full of affection. "There is good stuff at the dollar store these days," she defended herself.

As I watched them, I couldn't help but feel a pang of longing. This was what I wanted – a family, a home filled with love and laughter. And standing here with Eli, his hand in mine, I could almost imagine it.

I sucked in a slow breath, steeling myself for what was to come. Our families would be here soon, and everything would change. I just hoped it would be for the better.

The doorbell chimed, and my heart leaped into my throat. I squeezed Eli's hand, probably a bit too hard, but he didn't flinch. He just gave me that reas-suring smile that always made my knees weak.

"I'll get it," Nathan called, heading for the door.

As it swung open, I saw Harold and Patty Wells step inside. My stomach dropped like a kettlebell. Harold's eyes scanned the room, widening slightly when they landed on me. I could practically see the gears turning in his head.

"Carla?" he said, his voice gruff with surprise. "I didn't expect to see you here."

I swallowed hard. "Hi, Mr. Wells. Merry Christmas."

Patty, ever the peacemaker, stepped forward with a pie. "We brought dessert," she said, her voice warm despite the tension crackling in the air.

Harold's jaw tightened, his gaze flicking between Eli and me. I could feel Eli stiffen beside me, but before either of us could say anything, Nathan's boys came barreling into the room.

"Papa! Mimi!" they shouted, launching themselves at Harold and Patty.

The ice cracked, just a little. Harold's stern expression softened as he bent to hug his grandsons. "Hey there, troublemakers," he said, ruffling their hair.

I let out a breath. Maybe this wouldn't be so bad after all.

But then the doorbell rang again.

This time, Rebecca answered. "Jim, Trudy! Come on in," she said, ushering in my parents.

The moment my dad saw Harold, his face darkened. "What's going on here?" he demanded, looking around the room.

Harold straightened up, his eyes narrowing. "I was about to ask the same thing."

Oh boy. Here we go. I glanced at Eli, seeing my own worry reflected in his eyes. This was going to be one memorable Christmas gathering.

I felt Eli's hand tighten around mine, his palm slightly clammy. My heart raced as I watched him take a deep breath, his jaw clenching and unclenching. I gave his hand a gentle squeeze, hoping to convey all the support and love I couldn't put into words at that moment.

Eli cleared his throat, the sound cutting through the tense silence that had fallen over the room. All eyes turned to him, expectant and wary.

"Everyone," he began, his voice wavering slightly before finding its strength, "I have something important to say."

I could feel the weight of his father's gaze boring into us, but I kept my focus on Eli. He was trembling ever so slightly, but his eyes were determined.

"Carla and I are together," he announced, his voice ringing clear and true. "We're in love, and we're not going to let old grudges keep us apart anymore."

The room erupted in an array of reactions. My dad's face turned an alarming shade of red, while Harold's eyes bulged in disbelief.

"Absolutely not!" Harold bellowed, taking a menacing step forward. "Have you lost your mind, boy?"

My dad wasn't far behind. "Carla Marie Putnam, what do you think you're doing?" he demanded, his voice rising with each word.

I felt my own anger flaring up, but Eli squeezed my hand, reminding me we were in this together.

"We're not asking for permission," Eli said, a confidence I had rarely heard creeping into his voice. "We're telling you how it's going to be."

I couldn't help but smile, despite the situation. That was the Eli I knew and loved – brave, a little reckless, and always ready to stand up for what he believed in.

"You can't be serious," Harold scoffed, looking between us as if we'd grown second heads. "After everything that's happened between our families?"

"That's ancient history, Dad," Eli argued, his free hand clenching into a fist at his side. "Carla and I weren't even born when all that went down."

My dad shook his head vehemently. "It doesn't matter. A Wells is a Wells, and a Putnam is a Putnam. Oil and water, kiddo."

I felt a spark of defiance ignite in my chest. "Well, then call us salad dressing," I quipped, earning a surprised chuckle from Eli. "Because we're making it work."

The room fell silent, the tension so thick you could cut it with a knife. I held my breath, waiting for the next explosion.

I took a deep breath, squeezing Eli's hand for courage. "We know about my grandpa and Eli's Aunt Carol," I said softly, feeling the room grow still.

Harold's face paled, while my dad's eyes widened in shock. "He never–" he started, but I cut him off.

"Dad," I held up a hand and met his gaze, "he did. Grandma told me everything. Grandpa got Carol pregnant."

Dad shook his head. "No, he didn't. She lied!" But his voice lacked the determination of his earlier outburst.

"She didn't," I said, careful to keep my voice

steady. "Carol Wells was an eighteen-year-old girl. Whether she agreed to the affair or was coerced into it, Grandpa was the one who should have known better."

"You're sure?" he asked, his eyes on me.

I nodded, and my dad sank into the closest armchair. "But that means..." He glanced up at Harold. "My father? All these years—" His words broke off, thick with emotion. I watched as the color drained from both men's faces, decades of anger and resentment suddenly giving way to something else – was it shame?

I squeezed Eli's hand. "We understand that you both thought you were protecting your families. But don't you see? All this fighting, it's cost us all so much."

Eli interrupted, his voice steady despite the tremor I felt in his hand. "What matters is that both families are able to move forward."

My dad slumped into a nearby chair, suddenly looking every bit his age. "He always swore she was lying," he muttered, more to himself than to us.

Harold nodded slowly, his eyes meeting my dad's across the room. "Jim, I thought you knew—"

"That my dad had taken advantage of your sister?" my dad finished, a wry smile twisting his lips. "I'm so sorry, Harold. Oh my... Carol. The child. Where are they?" His questions came out rapidly.

"We'll sort it out, Jim." I was surprised to find the reassurance coming from Harold. "Carol gave the baby up for adoption – a little boy."

I sighed. I had an uncle I'd likely never meet, who also happened to be Eli's cousin. Talk about complicated.

I felt Eli relax slightly beside me, hope blooming in my chest. "It's time for secrets to end," I said softly. "We can walk through this. All of us, together."

The room fell silent again, but this time, it felt different. Less like a battlefield and more like... possibility.

I squeezed Eli's hand, drawing strength from his unwavering presence beside me. His dark eyes met mine, a silent conversation passing between us. We'd come this far; there was no turning back now.

"Look," Eli said, addressing both our fathers, "Carla and I love each other. We're not asking for your permission, but we'd really like your blessing."

I nodded, my voice steady as I added, "We're in this together, no matter what. But we want our families to be whole again."

I watched as Harold and my dad exchanged a long look. It wasn't quite forgiveness – not yet – but something had shifted. The tension in Harold's shoulders eased ever so slightly, and my dad's perpetual frown softened at the edges.

"You two are really serious about this, aren't you?" my dad asked, his voice gruff but not unkind.

I couldn't help the little laugh that escaped me. "Dad, we've been serious about this since high school. We just... couldn't act on it then."

Harold cleared his throat, adjusting his reading glasses. "I suppose... well, I suppose we haven't exactly made things easy for you kids."

"That's the understatement of the century, Dad," Eli quipped, but there was no malice in his tone.

I noticed Rebecca inching closer, a tentative smile on her face. "Maybe we could all use a fresh start," she suggested softly. "It is Christmas, after all."

The tension in the room seemed to dissipate further, like ice slowly melting under the warm glow of the Christmas lights. Nathan stepped forward, clapping a hand on Eli's shoulder. "I think that's a great idea, hon," he said, looking pointedly at Harold and my dad.

I held my breath, watching as the two men who had been at odds for so long regarded each other warily. Then, almost imperceptibly, my dad's lips twitched into what might have been the ghost of a smile.

"Well," he said, "I suppose stranger things have happened."

I felt Eli's hand tighten around mine as we both watched our fathers, hardly daring to breathe. Harold's weathered face creased with a mixture of emotions—reluctance, resignation, and something that looked suspiciously like hope.

"Then," my dad continued, clearing his throat, "I guess Harold and I better learn to get along. For your sakes."

Eli's arm slipped around my waist, pulling me close. "Does this mean we have your blessing?" he asked, his cocky grin barely concealing the vulnerability in his eyes.

Harold grunted, but I saw the corners of his mouth twitch. "Don't push me, boy. But... yes. If this is what makes you both happy, then you have my blessing."

"Mine too," my dad added.

I felt a rush of emotion so strong it nearly knocked me off my feet. Eli steadied me, his own eyes shining with unshed tears. "Thank you," I whispered, looking between our fathers. "Both of you."

As if on cue, Rebecca's boys chose that moment

to race through the room, shrieking with laughter. The spell of the moment broke, but in its place, a new warmth seemed to spread through the room.

I watched in amazement as Eli's mom hesitantly approached my own. "That pie smells wonderful," my mom said softly. "Maybe you could share the recipe?"

Eli's mom's face lit up. "Of course! It's an old family secret, but I suppose we're all family now, aren't we?"

As conversations began to bloom around us, Eli leaned in close, his breath warm against my ear. "Look at that," he murmured, nodding toward the room. Christmas lights twinkled merrily, casting a soft glow and reflecting off the windows.

I smiled, leaning into him. "We did it," I said. The sight of our families, tentatively beginning to mingle after so many years of feuding, was more beautiful than any decoration.

"Merry Christmas, Carla," Eli said softly, pressing a kiss to my temple.

I closed my eyes, savoring the moment. "Merry Christmas, Eli," I whispered back, feeling for the first time in years that the words truly meant something.

As the warm chatter of our families filled the

room, I allowed myself to hope that this was just the beginning of many more Christmases to come.

I LED Carla through the snowy path, her gloved hand warm in mine despite the frigid night air. Our breaths puffed out in little clouds as we walked, and I could feel the anticipation thrumming through her.

"Are we there yet?" she asked for the millionth time, a hint of laughter in her voice.

"Almost," I replied, grinning even though she couldn't see me through the blindfold. "Just a few more steps."

As we rounded the final bend, the glow of the small fire I'd set up earlier came into view. My heart stuttered in my chest.

"Okay," I said, stopping us both. "You can take off the blindfold now."

Carla reached up and tugged the fabric away from her eyes. For a moment, she just blinked, taking in the scene before her. Then her eyes widened, reflecting the dancing flames.

"Eli," she breathed. "This is... wow."

I'd spread out a thick blanket near the fire, with a thermos of hot cocoa and a basket of snacks waiting.

Raccoon Lake stretched out beyond us, its surface glassy and still under the starry sky.

"You like it?" I asked, suddenly feeling a bit nervous. What if she thought it was cheesy?

But Carla's smile was radiant as she turned to me. "I love it. But how did you manage all this?"

I rubbed the back of my neck, sheepish. "Well, I had some help. Your parents are up at the house, actually. They set everything up for me."

Carla's eyebrows shot up. "My parents? Really?"

"Yeah." I chuckled. "Turns out they don't hate me as much as I thought."

As we settled onto the blanket, I couldn't help but marvel at how far we'd come. From clandestine meetings under the bleachers to this moment, with our families finally starting to come around. It felt like a small miracle.

Carla's voice pulled me from my thoughts. "This is really beautiful, Eli. Thank you."

I looked at her, the firelight casting a warm glow on her face, and felt my heart swell. Maybe I wasn't such a screw-up after all. I pulled Carla close, savoring her warmth as we leaned against each other. The cocoa was rich and comforting as we sipped it, our breaths mingling in the frosty air.

"You know," I said, breaking the comfortable

silence, "if someone had told me a year ago we'd be sitting here like this, I'd have laughed in their face."

Carla chuckled, the sound warming me more than the fire. "Me too." She was quiet, and I could practically hear the gears turning in her head. "Eli, can I tell you something?"

"Anything," I said, meaning it more than I ever had before.

She took a deep breath. "I've been thinking a lot about our families lately. This reconciliation... it's like a weight I didn't even know I was carrying has been lifted."

I nodded, encouraging her to continue.

"It's just... for so long, loving you felt like I was betraying my family somehow. But now?" Carla's eyes met mine, shining with unshed tears. "Now it feels like we're free. Like we can finally just be us, you know?"

My heart gave a giddy leap, betraying my cool exterior. Carla had just said she loved me. I wanted to hear it over and over again. Maybe I could have her record it on my phone. I'd make it my ringtone.

I pulled her closer and pressed a kiss to her temple. "I know exactly what you mean," I murmured, marveling at how far we'd come and how much further we could go, together.

I took a deep breath, feeling a surge of emotion I'd rarely allowed myself to experience, let alone express. "Carla, I... I can't even begin to tell you how grateful I am for you. For your support, your patience..." I trailed off, searching for the right words. "You've seen me at my worst, and you've never given up on me."

My mind flashed back to all the times I'd pushed her away, all the stupid stunts I'd pulled to prove I didn't need anyone. To prove I didn't need her. I had been dead wrong. I needed her like I needed air.

"You know, becoming a firefighter was supposed to be about proving something to my dad," I admitted, my voice low. "But somewhere along the way, it became about proving something to myself."

Carla's hand found mine, her fingers intertwining with my own. "I've always seen the good in you, even when you couldn't see it yourself."

I felt a lump forming in my throat. "I don't think I realized how important you were to me until I almost lost you. I was such an idiot."

Carla laughed softly, the sound warming me more than the fire ever could. "Well, I can't argue with that," she teased, before her expression turned serious. "But, Eli, the man you've become... I'm in awe of him."

I raised an eyebrow, trying to lighten the mood. "Even with all my dorky dad jokes?"

"Especially with those," she replied, her eyes twinkling. "Do you remember that cocky boy in high school who thought he could solve every problem by flashing a grin and flexing his muscles?"

I groaned. "Please, don't remind me."

"He's still in there," Carla said, poking my chest gently. "But now he's part of this incredible man who runs into burning buildings to save people, who's working on mending fences with his family, who's..." she paused, her voice softening, "who's not afraid to be vulnerable anymore."

I felt my cheeks flush, and for once, it wasn't from the cold. "I'm still working on that last part," I admitted.

"I know," Carla said, squeezing my hand. "And that's what I admire most. You're trying, Eli. You're growing. And I'm so proud of the man you've become."

I swallowed hard, feeling a lump form in my throat. Carla's words hit me like a ton of bricks, but in the best way possible. I gazed at her, taking in the way the firelight danced across her face, highlighting the flecks of gold in her dark eyes.

Around us, the night was alive with a gentle

symphony. The fire crackled softly, sending sparks spiraling into the inky sky. Above, stars twinkled like a million tiny diamonds, their light reflecting off the still surface of Raccoon Lake.

My heart raced as I realized what I wanted – no, needed – to say. This was it. I had to tell her everything. I was in so far head over my heels for this girl, I wouldn't ever hide it again.

"Carla," I began, taking her hands in mine. My palms were sweaty, and I prayed she wouldn't notice. "I know I'm not perfect. I'm probably the farthest thing from it. But being with you... it makes me want to be better."

I paused, searching for the right words. How could I possibly express everything she meant to me?

"I promise," I continued, my voice thick with emotion, "to always cherish you. To support you through whatever life throws our way. Whether it's feuding families or burning buildings, I'll be right there beside you."

As I spoke, I couldn't help but think, 'Is this really me? The guy who used to run from commitment faster than a four-alarm fire?' But looking into Carla's eyes, I knew. This wasn't just me – this was the best version of me, the one she brought out.

Carla's eyes glistened in the firelight as she squeezed my hands. For a moment, I worried I'd said too much, but then she spoke, her voice soft yet resolute.

"Oh, Eli," she began, a tremor in her voice. "You've always been more than you give yourself credit for. I promise to stand by your side, through every up and down. To nurture this love we've fought so hard for."

My heart swelled as she continued, "I'll be your biggest cheerleader, your partner in crime, and the one to knock some sense into that thick skull of yours when needed."

I couldn't help but chuckle at that last part. Classic Carla, wrapping sincerity in sass.

"I vow to love you, Elijah Wells, not despite your flaws, but because of them. They're part of what makes you... you."

As she spoke, I felt a warmth spread through me that had nothing to do with the nearby fire. This was real.

The clock on my watch ticked closer to midnight, and a palpable sense of anticipation filled the air. Carla and I exchanged glances, hope and excitement dancing in our eyes like the flickering flames beside us.

"So," I said, my trademark grin spreading across my face, "ready to start the new year right?"

Carla rolled her eyes, but I could see the smile she was trying to hide. "With you? I'm ready for anything."

As we sat there, hands intertwined, I couldn't help but think how far we'd come. Our journey had been anything but smooth. Yet here we were, stronger for it all.

Suddenly, the sky erupted in a burst of color. Brilliant reds, greens, and golds exploded overhead, their reflections dancing across the surface of Raccoon Lake. I felt Carla's hand tighten in mine as we both gazed upward, mouths agape.

"Eli," she breathed, her eyes wide with wonder, "did you plan this too?"

I chuckled, shaking my head. "For once, I can't take credit. But man, talk about perfect timing."

As we watched the fireworks paint the night sky, I couldn't help but draw parallels to our relationship. Each burst of light seemed to represent a moment in our shared history—the highs and lows, the arguments and reconciliations, all leading to this breathtaking display.

"You know," I said, leaning in close to be heard over the booming explosions, "I used to think our relationship was like a house fire— intense, unpre-dictable, and likely to leave everything in ashes."

Carla turned to me, one eyebrow raised. "Seri-ously? That's your romantic analogy?"

I grinned, undeterred. "Let me finish. Now, looking at these fireworks, I realize I was wrong. We're not destruction; we're celebration. We're bright, and yeah, maybe a little loud and chaotic, but ultimately, we're something beautiful."

As I spoke, I saw Carla's expression soften. She squeezed my hand, and I felt a surge of hope for our future. The air around us seemed charged with possibility, each colorful explosion overhead rein-forcing the promise of new beginnings.

I turned to face Carla, my heart pounding so hard I was sure she could hear it over the fireworks. Her eyes sparkled, reflecting the kaleidoscope of colors above us. I cupped her face gently with my free hand, my thumb tracing her cheekbone.

"Carla," I whispered, my voice thick with emotion, "I love you. I always have, and I always will."

She smiled, tears glistening in her eyes. "I love you too, Eli. Despite everything... or maybe because of it."

I leaned in, pressing my lips to hers in a tender

kiss. It felt like coming home after years of wandering. The fireworks crescendoed around us, as if nature itself was celebrating our reunion. I poured every ounce of love, every promise, every hope for our future into that kiss.

When we finally pulled apart, breathless, the last of the fireworks faded from the sky. The sudden quiet was profound, broken only by the soft crackling of our little fire. I wrapped my arm around Carla's shoulders, pulling her close as we settled back onto the blanket.

I grinned, feeling invincible. The warmth of the fire, the lingering taste of Carla's kiss, the weight of her against me – it all felt surreal, like a dream I never wanted to wake from.

"You know," Carla murmured, her gloved fingers idly tracing patterns on my chest, "I used to daydream about moments like this with you. But the reality? So much better."

I kissed the top of her head, inhaling the scent of her shampoo. "Agreed. Though I gotta say, in my daydreams, I was way smoother and didn't nearly trip over my own feet leading you down the path."

Her quiet laughter warmed me more than any fire could. As we lay there, enveloped in our little cocoon of warmth and love, I felt a sense of peace I'd never known before. Whatever challenges we'd face, whatever obstacles life threw our way, I knew we'd face them together.

No matter what I had to give up to be with Carla, I'd risk it all in a heartbeat.

Epilogue

CARLA

I stood at the edge of Minden Park, my heart doing a happy dance as I scanned the bustling crowd. The vibrant energy of the town fair surrounded me, a cheerful reminder of how far we'd come. My eyes searched for him, the man who—against all odds—had become my everything.

Adjusting my sundress, I felt a familiar flutter of excitement. Eli and I had faced down family feuds, misunderstandings, and years of tension to get to this point. Now, with all of that behind us, today was just about fun and celebration.

Taking a deep breath, I stepped into the crowd. Mrs. Henderson waved at me from her craft booth, and I returned her greeting with a bright smile. "Those quilts look amazing, Mrs. H!"

"Thank you, dear," she called back. "And you're looking radiant!"

I laughed, the warmth in her words matching the sunlight streaming through the trees. This was home—the place where everyone knew you, and life felt like a patchwork quilt of love and laughter.

As I neared the bake sale booth, Rebecca spotted me and grinned. "Looking for someone special?" she teased.

I rolled my eyes, but my smile gave me away. "Just enjoying the day."

"Mmm-hmm," Rebecca said knowingly. "Well, a certain firefighter might be looking for you too."

My heart skipped a beat as I thanked her and made my way toward the auction stage. The colorful banners and cheerful music created a lively backdrop for the event. My gaze swept over the stage, and there he was—Elijah Wells, standing tall and confident in his firefighter uniform, the sunlight catching the easy grin that never failed to steal my breath.

As if sensing my gaze, Eli looked out over the crowd. When his eyes found mine, a slow smile spread across his face, and the world around us seemed to blur.

"Ladies and gentlemen," the auctioneer's booming

voice called out, snapping me back to reality, "it's time to bid on a date with one of our newest hometown heroes. Introducing Evan Mercer! He just moved here from Chicago and we're lucky to have him joining the MRFD as a new firefighter! Do I have $50?"

Paddles flew up in the air as community members bid on the opportunity to personally welcome Evan to town. But my eyes were entirely fixed on Eli, standing in the background, waiting for his turn.

Eli's eyes sparkled with mischief as he gave a playful wave. As four hours with Evan Mercer was sold to the highest bidder, I couldn't contain my happiness. The past five months with Eli had been everything I ever wanted.

"Up next, we have Elijah Wells. To know him is to love this Minden native."

My heart thumped as the bidding began.

"Do I hear $50?" the auctioneer called.

Paddles shot up, and I quickly joined in. Eli's amused expression turned into something softer, something just for me. With each bid, I felt the excitement build—not just for the auction, but for the moment I knew was coming. I wasn't going to let anyone else steal my time with my firefighter.

"$500!" I called out, my voice steady despite the pounding of my heart. The auctioneer called for further bids, but the crowd fell silent. The town of Minden was solidly behind us as our families had put the feud to rest.

The crowd erupted in cheers as the auctioneer declared, "Sold! $500 to Miss Carla Putnam!"

Eli stepped off the stage, weaving through the crowd until he was standing in front of me. His grin was brighter than the sun as he took my hand. "Quite the bid there, Putnam. You must really want that date."

"Maybe I just didn't want anyone else to have you," I teased, my cheeks warming.

Eli's gaze softened as he reached into his pocket and pulled out a small velvet box. The world seemed to tilt as he dropped to one knee. This was really happening?

"Carla," he began, his voice steady but filled with emotion, "I'm pretty glad you bid on me. No one else gets to have me, because I don't want to give this ring to anybody else. You've become my best friend, my fiercest ally, and the love of my life. Will you marry me?"

Tears blurred my vision as I nodded, unable to

speak past the lump in my throat. "Yes, Eli. Of course, yes!"

Cheers erupted around us as Eli slipped the ring onto my finger and stood, pulling me into his arms. Our kiss was met with applause and laughter, a perfect reflection of the joy we felt in that moment.

As the crowd celebrated around us, Eli leaned close, his voice low and full of promise. "This is just the beginning, Carla."

I smiled, my heart full. "The beginning of our forever."

Epilogue

SAMANTHA BROWN

"Mom, hurry up!" Sophia tugged on my hand, her dark curls bouncing as she skipped ahead. At thirteen, she still had a boundless enthusiasm for events like this — cotton candy, games, all her friends from school. The Spring Sparks Auction was the place to be in Minden in May.

I smiled at her. "I'm coming, kiddo. Slow down before you run into someone." My shift at the library's booth was done and Sophia was itching to socialize.

Sophia rolled her eyes but slowed her pace. "You always worry too much. It's just Minden. What could possibly go wrong?"

Plenty, I thought but didn't say aloud. That was

my job. I was the one who had to protect her. She was innocent in the ways of the world. The way one mistake could change the course of your entire life.

We wove through the crowd, passing familiar faces. Some smiled and waved, while others paused for quick pleasantries. Sophia was the social butterfly. Had I been that way once? Perhaps. But that was a long time ago. More than thirteen years, in fact. Finding out you were single and pregnant at nineteen years old would do that to a girl.

The auction stage loomed ahead, and Sophia's excitement ratcheted up another notch. "Can we stay for the firefighter auction? Please? I want to see who bids on them."

I hesitated. The firefighter auction was always entertaining – the men were goofballs, honestly. But I got anxious being in the middle of a crowd. Like something would spiral out of control like it had—

I shook away the thought. This wasn't Panama City and I wasn't under the influence of anything.

Sophia was looking at me with those pleading eyes that made it impossible to say no.

"Fine," I relented. "But we're not staying long. I have a lot to do at home."

Sophia grinned and pulled me closer to the stage.

We found a spot near the back, where the crowd wasn't as dense, and settled in to watch.

The auctioneer's booming voice echoed through the square, drawing cheers and laughter from the audience. One by one, the firefighters took the stage, lining up along the back like some cheesy calendar spread.

Instead of looking at them, I was scanning the crowd when I heard the auctioneer announce a new name.

"Evan Mercer! He just moved here from Chicago and we're lucky to have him joining the MRFD as a new firefighter? Do I have $50?"

My heart stopped.

No. No, it couldn't be.

I turned toward the stage, and there he was. Evan Mercer, standing tall and confident, his expression warm and easy as he waved at the crowd.

The world seemed to tilt beneath my feet. My mind raced, the years unraveling in an instant. The memories hit me like a freight train—his smile, his laugh, the lights, and the deafening music.

The night that had changed everything.

I swallowed hard, my breath coming in short, shallow bursts. What was he doing here? In Minden, of all places?

"Mom? Are you okay?" Sophia's voice pulled me back to the present. She was watching me with concern, her brow furrowed.

"I'm fine," I lied, forcing a tight smile. "Just enjoying the show."

Sophia turned her attention back to the stage, but my mind was spinning. This couldn't be happening. Evan Mercer—the man I'd kept a secret from for thirteen years—was here, in my hometown.

The bids climbed higher, the crowd cheering as Evan's time was auctioned off to the highest bidder. He seemed oblivious to my presence, his attention focused on the stage.

Good. He didn't know I was here. Not that he probably even remembered me. It wasn't as if he had ever called the number I'd given him. It had just been one night for him. One that I had lived the consequences of for thirteen years. I wouldn't trade Sophia for anything. But Evan didn't even know she existed.

But how long would that last? Minden wasn't a big town. It was only a matter of time before our paths crossed, and when they did, he would see Sophia.

Sophia, who had his eyes. His smile. His curiosity.

I clenched my hands into fists, my nails digging into my palms. I had made my choice all those years ago, a choice I had agonized over. I'd looked him up. Evan Mercer. Eldest son of Sterling Mercer. I probably should have recognized the name when he'd given it to me. But I was nineteen. I wasn't exactly reading the *Wall Street Journal*.

Telling Evan about the pregnancy had seemed impossible at the time. I didn't know how to contact him. We were both young, our relationship barely more than a fleeting connection. And after I realized who he was? If the Mercer family found out about Evan's indiscretion... They'd take Sophia away from me. And there was no way I would let that happen. It was better this way—for him, for me, for Sophia.

But now, with Evan here in Minden, of all places, the fragile peace I had built was teetering on the edge of collapse.

I glanced at Sophia, her face lit up with excitement as the auctioneer called for bids on another firefighter. She had no idea. No idea that the man walking down the stairs of the stage was her father.

A fresh wave of guilt washed over me, threatening to drown me. Sophia deserved to know the truth. Lord knew she'd asked enough questions about her father over the years.

Evan deserved to know the truth, too. But how could I upend his life now, after all this time?

The crowd erupted into cheers, jolting me out of my thoughts. I looked back at the stage just in time to see a woman in a sundress make her way forward. The crowd parted for her, their cheers growing louder.

"Sold! $500 to Miss Carla Putnam!" the auctioneer declared.

I knew Carla, of course. Seeing her with Eli Wells around town was nothing new over the last several months. They'd even come into the library while I worked one day for some sort of scavenger hunt date he'd created.

And now, she was walking up to Elijah Wells with a winning bid and a radiant smile.

My gaze shifted to Elijah, who stood off to the side, his eyes fixed on Carla with a look of pure adoration.

For a brief moment, my anxiety took a backseat to envy. The way Eli looked at Carla was...everything.

But then my eyes found Evan again, and the weight of reality came crashing back down.

I needed to get out of here.

"Sophia," I said, my voice sharper than I intended, "we should go."

"But the auction's not over yet!" she protested.

"I have a headache," I said. "Let's go grab some lemonade and head home."

Sophia frowned but didn't argue. As we made our way through the crowd, I kept my head down, praying Evan wouldn't see me.

This wasn't just about me anymore. This was about Sophia, her life, and the secret I had kept for so long.

I had to figure out what to do—how to protect her, how to face Evan, how to tell the truth after thirteen years of silence.

But as I glanced back at the stage one last time, I couldn't shake the feeling that everything was about to change – again.

SECOND CHANCE FIRE Station

Get Samantha and Evan's story now in **The One Who Changed Everything.**

Available now!

Note to Readers

Thank you for picking up (or downloading!) this book. If you enjoyed it, please consider taking a minute to leave a review or rating! It makes a world of difference for independent authors like myself. I loved writing Carla and Elijah... but I'm even more excited for Samantha and Evan's story!

I hope you recognize how Carla and Eli's faith impacted their journey. Struggling to trust the Lord and seeking His wisdom when there doesn't seem to be a good "right" answer. And – for every book in this Second Chance Fire Station series; the understanding that God's timing is perfect, even when it is slower than we would hope... it is never late.

I pray my books encourage you in your faith and through your struggles, whatever they may be. I love hearing the amazing ways God has used my words in the lives of my readers. It is incredibly humbling and encouraging! You can email me anytime at tara graceericson@gmail.com.

You can also learn more about my upcoming projects at my website: www.taragraceericson.com or by signing up for my newsletter there. Just for signing up, you'll get two free ebooks and the audio-book of Hawthorne Bloom's story in Hoping for Hawthorne.

Thank you again for all your support and encouragement.

Acknowledgments

Jesus, I love you. Thank you for your grace upon grace in my life. I offer this book to you – use it for your kingdom in ways beyond what I could ask or imagine.

Thank you to Lindsay Nickel Photography for the rights and Mark and Kristen Boutros for letting me use their beautiful photo on the cover. Wishing you many years of happiness together!

To the "real" Carla – Watching your happily ever after is my favorite. Thanks for letting me be real with you.

To Jessica from New Life Editing Solutions… my partner in crime. It's been a journey over the last six years, but I'm so glad we get to do parts of it together.

To my copy editor – Brandi from Editing Done Write. Thank you for your encouragement, flexibility, and for fixing all my tenses and comma errors! One of these days, I'll have a book done when I promised it to you.

To Hannah Jo Abbott and Mandi Blake. Just...
Thanks.

And to the rest of our Author Circle -- Jess
Mastorakos, Elizabeth Maddrey and K Leah. No one
is allowed to leave the tribe. Sorry. You're stuck
with us.

To my parents, for being a wonderful example of
love, faith, and hard work. The longer I am a parent,
the more I recognize how wonderful the two of you
were at it.

To Tiffany, Megan, Jessica, Laurie, Dulcie, Tawni,
Donna Marie, Bethany, and all the Christian
Mommy Writers. Thanks for spurring me on... and
for all the hours in the Zoom room.

Thank you to all my readers, without whose
support and encouragement, I would have given up
a long time ago.

To all the other bloggers, bookstagrammers, and
reviewers who read my books and share your
thoughts. Thank you from the bottom of my heart.
Special thanks to the members of my street team for
helping launch this book into the world. It's so much
more fun to release a book with a cheering section.

And finally, to my husband. I can't relate to
Carla's parents' disapproval of Elijah, because my
parents have loved you from day one... You're the

biggest green flag. I wouldn't want to do this with anyone else.

Mr. B – I've loved all our time together this year. Keep seeking the Lord, embracing yourself, and loving others.

Little C – Can you stop growing up so fast? I love you so much.

And Baby L – I probably shouldn't call you a baby anymore, but you'll always be mine. Love you.

About the Author

Tara Grace Ericson lives in Missouri with her husband and three sons. She studied engineering and worked as an engineer for many years before embracing her creative side to become a full-time author. Now, she spends her days chasing her boys and writing books when she can.

She loves cooking, crocheting, and reading books by the dozen. She loves a good "happily ever after" with an engaging love story. That's why Tara focuses on writing clean contemporary romance, with an emphasis on Christian faith and living. She wants to encourage her readers with stories of men and women who live out their faith in tough situations.

Second Chance Fire Station

THE ONE WHO CHANGED EVERYTHING

That one night changed their lives. When their worlds collide again, he discovers what he lost, and what he'll fight to keep.

I never meant to leave her.

But when she disappeared after that night, I convinced myself it was for the best. Love wasn't meant for a man carrying this much guilt.

Then I came to Minden, looking for a fresh start, only to find *her*—Samantha, the woman I never forgot. And with her? A daughter I never knew existed.

Samantha isn't happy to see me. In fact, she wants nothing to do with me. As much as I want to hate her for keeping my daughter from me, I can't blame her.

I lost my brother that night. I won't lose them, too.

Now, I have a second chance, but Samantha doesn't trust me. I don't blame her. My past, my name, my family—everything she ran from, I represent. But I won't walk away again.

Even if it means facing the past I've spent years trying to outrun. Because no matter how much time has passed, she's still **The One Who Changed Everything.**

Now Available!

Books by Tara Grace Ericson

Free Stories

Love and Chocolate

Clean Slate (Romantic Suspense)

Black Tower Security

Potential Threat

Hostile Intent

Critical Witness

Imminent Danger

Second Chance Fire Station

The One Who Got Away

The One She Can't Forget

The One Who Promised Forever

The Bloom Sisters Series

Hoping for Hawthorne - A Bloom Family Novella

A Date for Daisy

Poppy's Proposal

Lavender and Lace

Longing for Lily

Resisting Rose

Dancing with Dandelion

Heroes of Freedom Ridge (multi-author series)

Forgiven by the Hero

Believing the Hero (2022 Carol Award Finalist)

Blind Date with the Hero

Seasons of Love Series

Falling on Main Street

Winter Wishes

Spring Fever

Summer to Remember

Kissing in the Kitchen: Series Bonus Novella